THE
SECOND
THIEF

TRAVIS
THRASHER

MOODY PUBLISHERS
CHICAGO

Scripture quotations are taken from *The Living Bible*
copyright © 1971. Used by permission of Tyndale House
Publishers, Inc., Wheaton, Illinois 60189. All rights
reserved.

Scripture marked KJV are taken from the King James
Version.

Library of Congress Cataloging-in-publication Data

Thrasher, Travis, 1971–
  The second thief / Travis Thrasher.
    p. cm.
  ISBN 0-8024-1707-8
  1. Survival after airplane accidents, shipwrecks, etc.—
    Fiction. I.
  Title.
  PS3570.H6925 S43 2003
  813'.6—dc21

3 5 7 9 10 8 6 4 2

Printed in the United States of America

To my sister, Laura, for always showing me the way.

With special thanks to the following:

Sharon, Dad, Mom, Anne Christian Buchanan, Michele Straubel, Greg Thornton, and Ron Beers. Without your help this book wouldn't have been possible.

Then he said, "Jesus, remember me when you come into your Kingdom."

Luke 23:42

❖   ❖   ❖

Y ou sure you know where you're going?"

The man in back of the cab tells the driver yes, then says take the next right. The road ends at a cul-de-sac.

"Right here is fine," says the passenger.

The driver turns and glares back at him, squinting at the light gray uniform and the badge that reads Mardell Services. "What're you gonna do here?"

"I'm meeting someone."

Twenty dollars takes care of the fare. Once the taxi purrs away, its orange glare fading into darkness, the uniformed man turns on a flashlight and begins to sprint through the woods that edge the dead-end road.

In fifteen minutes, he is standing on the north lawn of a sprawling six-story office building. The modern structure appears to be made entirely out of glass, as if a strategically hurled rock could shatter it. The lit parking lot is empty save a van parked at the front of the entrance.

He slows his breathing and takes off his cap, wiping the sweat from his forehead. He readjusts his glasses as he slips back on the cap and walks toward the entrance of the building.

He taps on the glass doors for a couple of minutes. A round man in his fifties finally moves behind the front desk and ambles over to open the door.

"Yeah?" he asks in a sluggish tone as the door slides open.

"Missed my ride," the uniformed man says, pointing to the van.

"With the cleaners?"

The man nods, showing him the photo badge he wears.

"They came in about fifteen minutes ago."

"I'll find them."

The uninterested security man lets him pass and takes his place back on his cushioned chair.

The uniformed man rubs his weekend's worth of dark beard and finds the elevator.

❖　　　❖　　　❖

The metal doors open to darkness, and Tom Ledger steps out to commit a felony. He doesn't look around, doesn't hesitate, doesn't notice any irregularities in his breathing. His tennis shoes, wet from the damp grass outside, brush the office carpet without sound. It takes him just a couple of minutes to find the cubicle close to the men's room against the south side. Sitting in the chair, he reaches down and turns on the computer.

The monitor sheds light on the drab and tidy holding cell, illuminating the nameplate on the desk next to a *Star Wars* action figure: *Calvin Morris*. While the operating system loads, he locates Calvin's stash of high-capacity zip disks and slips one of the disks into the appropriate drive.

The computer asks for a password, and he types it in without thought.

Boba Fett.

He waits until the screen icons are all in place, ready for action. Then he accesses the file system and searches.

The files he wants are labeled Coverter45-78, 79, 80, and 81. He saves them onto the disk as Vacations #1, 2, 3, and 4, then slips the disk into his shirt pocket.

He shuts down the computer and heads back for the elevator. He can hear the cleaning crew in the distance, but he ignores the voices as he presses the Up button once again.

The sixth floor is as dark as the fourth floor was, but Tom doesn't need a light. A thousand mornings he's walked this route and can do it blindfolded. With illuminated crimson exit boxes creating the only shadows, he skirts another maze of cubicles to enter the western corner office.

He reaches in his pants pocket and takes out a mint, finishing it in two quick bites.

A quick glance at his watch tells him it's quarter after two, three or four hours before the first morning brown-noser starts the first office pot of coffee. He himself generally arrives around nine, leaving anywhere from six to nine or ten, depending on how many stupid meetings kept him from doing any actual work.

He taps his shirt pocket as he crosses to the desk and opens his Sony laptop. No more meetings after tonight. This will be his last hour at Hammett-Korning Technologies.

The Sony flickers through its start-up ritual, and

Tom glances around the office he hopes never to lay eyes on again. In the cold glow of the LCD's light, he surveys the surroundings of half a decade past and feels nothing. He sees the outline of his head and shoulders on the framed poster on the wall in front of him, a picture of a climber ascending a mountain with the slogan in glorious bold urging all to "Seize the Day!"

He hates this poster and the other fifty like it that litter the various floors of Hammett-Korning. To him, they've always symbolized a human resources department not doing its job. Motivating jingles don't compensate for corporate indifference and executive incompetence.

How's this for seizing the day? Tom thinks.

He gets into his email system and finds the carefully worded email he's already prepared. He rereads it before clicking to send it off. The message is satisfying and succinct:

"Dear Bob. I quit."

Tom scans the list of unread emails that have accumulated and feels a sense of relief at never having to read any more memos on testing standards and new procedures and endless, technological rhetoric he never wanted to have anything to do with in the first place. This job had always been about one thing: money. And he finally realized a while ago that there was no pot of gold at the end of the Hammett-Korning rainbow.

Except possibly on the disk in his pocket. He attaches an external drive to the laptop, slips in the disk from Calvin's office, and verifies that the vacation documents are still there. Still tucked away on the disk as Vacations 1, 2, 3, and 4.

Thank you, Calvin.

It doesn't take long to upload the files to the laptop, download them again to the tiny memory stick in his Sony's media slot, then wipe them from the disk and the laptop's hard drive.

He slips out the memory stick. It's a little over an inch long and almost half as wide. Tom tucks the slender device into his wallet like a memento and feels no difference when he slides the wallet back in his pants pocket. Then he unplugs the zip drive and powers down the laptop.

Glancing around, making sure he collects everything he needs, Tom notices the frame on the edge of his desk. He picks it up and stares at it, the picture hard to see in the dim light. He can picture it in his sleep, however. It's a photo of Allegra. For a while he kept it as a front, a picture to portray a life he didn't lead. He can admit to himself that he kept it for other reasons too. He is not one to wallow in the past or to get sentimental over could-have-beens. The photo is simply a reminder of a different time. Proof that a brighter day existed.

He slips the photo out of the frame and into his pocket. Then, without a further thought, he exits the office and heads for the stairs.

❖   ❖   ❖

The first-floor lights are on and the cleaning crew noise is louder, but nobody sees Tom as he pushes open a door and steps out to the shipping area at the back of the Hammett-Korning building. This is where they send and receive mail, packages, shipments—anything that's coming or going. He was down here earlier in the day,

11

looking around, scoping out the territory. As he walked around here in blue slacks and a yellow tie, looking corporate and professional, he wondered how many people even knew who he was. Just another suit, one employee out of a thousand.

More important, he wondered if anyone had a clue *what* he was going to do. He's pretty sure no one even noticed him.

The exit door next to the trucking bays has one of those push bars that let people out but not in. Tom has already checked that exiting here doesn't trigger an alarm. The door barely makes a noise as it closes behind him.

Emerging under the clear night sky, he realizes he's done it. Just as simple as he thought it would be. Nobody knows. Not even good ol' Bob.

He thinks of Hammett-Korning—the company he's leaving behind, the company he's stealing from—and feels nothing. How will a little corporate theft make any difference? The company has three more offices in the surrounding area. Tens of thousands of employees. A monstrous megacompany run by a CEO who's been showing up in the news. A CEO who might be in jail before too long.

He emerges from the building's shadow and walks down the street for about half a mile. In another deserted parking lot outside a two-story office building, a lone car waits for him. The black Porsche Boxster parked next to a streetlamp reflects his form as he nears.

Inside the car, he flips open a cell phone and makes a call. He knows it will go straight to voice mail.

"It's done. See you tonight at six sharp."

❖   ❖   ❖

If you knew you were about to die and could call me, what would your final words be?"

Tom looks across the room at the lanky blonde who asked the question. Her short hair is wet from the shower. She's watching some sort of TV newscast.

He grins and goes back to reading the paper, standing at the island of the condo's kitchen.

"What was that look for?" she asks, no longer focusing on the television.

"That's a big assumption."

"What? That you'd die?"

"That I'd call you."

She makes a face at him but he just smiles, rubs his freshly shaven face, then finishes the glass of grapefruit juice and places it in the kitchen sink.

Janine turns back to the story about a man in California who called his wife from the scene of a bank robbery moments before he was shot to death.

"Isn't that awful?" she asks.

"Quite."

"So you wouldn't call me?"

"I don't think I'd want to draw attention to myself

during a bank robbery."

"But what would you say if you could?"

Tom Ledger looks at the morning beauty in the white terry-cloth robe, shakes his head, and crosses the room to give her a good-bye kiss on the neck. She is used to his not answering questions such as this.

"Will you call?" she asks.

"Of course." He knows this is a lie.

"By the way . . . where'd you go last night?"

A suitcase and matching briefcase rest by the door to Janine's one-bedroom condo.

"Just went out to get some air," he says. Another lie.

"Air? At like two in the morning?"

"Sure. Couldn't sleep, so I went out."

"I heard the garage door open around three. Is everything okay?"

He nods. Everything's perfect.

"You've been kinda on the moody side the last couple days. Even last night—"

"The limo's here."

She pauses, and he knows that she knows better than to push it.

"Have a great trip."

He picks up his bags and walks out the door. He has known Janine for over two months. She's six years younger than his thirty-four years and around a dozen younger in terms of maturity. Some might question what he is doing with her in the first place and exactly how much maturity that shows, but Tom doesn't care.

He won't be seeing her again anyway.

❖   ❖   ❖

He leans back in the leather seat of the Town Car as it heads for O'Hare International Airport. He thinks of Janine's question.

"What would your final words be?"

If he could call anyone, who would he call anyway? Not Janine. The obvious answer occurs to him. But he knows Allegra wouldn't accept a call from him or allow him to get out five words. And no one else comes to mind.

Vacations 1, 2, 3, and 4 echo in his head. He thinks of making the California trip a quick one, then maybe going down to Florida and finally getting to see the Keys and losing himself down there for a while. A month. A year. He's not entirely sure.

The landscape of suburbia blurs by him. Street upon street upon store upon subdivision. He passes the time by comparing this northern suburb of Chicago with what he knows of Key West. He knows the Keys are probably not that different from Wood Grove or any other location. It probably has its share of secrets, its ugly little realities. And it also has its share of people trying to ease the pain of living with their mistakes.

The difference is that, in a place like Key West, you have ocean sunsets to make it all a little easier.

❖   ❖   ❖

Tom waits in an airport bar drinking a club soda with lime. Around him sit passengers who are either about to board or just getting off a plane, most of them laughing and drinking and having a good time. He finds locales such as this comforting. He can sit alone, and as long as he appears to be drinking something heavy and continues to tip the bartender enough, he can remain unbothered.

The phone at his side vibrates.

"Yeah."

"It's me."

"Yeah," Tom says again, recognizing the male voice.

"That easy, huh?"

"Told you. Been there long enough to know what it's like."

"Are you sure no one knows?"

"Very few people would even have a clue as to what is really valuable inside. And how to get it."

"So you got everything?"

"You'll see it tonight."

"We'll have to celebrate. Dinner's on me."

"That won't be the only thing."

The man on the other end laughs, and Tom hangs up.

He sips his drink and stares to his right at the passengers shuffling between gates. A family of four meanders past, and he studies them. A man about his age with light-brown hair and a well-worn sports coat. A pretty but tired-looking wife in a conservative, flowing skirt and a jeans vest over a white T-shirt. The woman holds a baby against her shoulder while the man links hands with a little girl, perhaps four or five.

Soon they're out of view, and Tom resumes being invisible. His thoughts shift to pondering the type of yacht he'll be purchasing in the next few weeks. He has narrowed it down to three. The choice will be an important one.

T wo aisles cut through the 767. Tom heads down the one on his right after stepping onto the plane and takes the aisle seat numbered 17B. He shoves his briefcase into the overhead bin along with his sports coat. The memory stick remains in his wallet. Looking through the oval window, he sees the long, sleek wing shining in the morning sunlight.

Normally Tom travels first class, but he normally travels on business and books well ahead of time. This was the only seat left on the 10:30 A.M. flight to San Francisco when he called a few days ago. He finds himself wishing for the space and privacy of the first-class seats ahead of him. As strangers pass, he wonders who will occupy the lone seat between him and the window.

A man laboring with a large suitcase stops next to Tom's row. He struggles with his piece of luggage as he tries to fit it in the overhead bin.

"Sorry," he says to the people behind him as he tries to jam it in.

Tom gets a clear look at his face and recognizes the family man he saw with the wife and two kids. The stranger carries a cordial grin even though he knows he's holding up the line.

A carrying case slips off the man's shoulder and lands in Tom's lap.

"Oh, sorry. Excuse me."

Tom says nothing but takes the black canvas bag, the sort they hand out free at conventions, and puts it in the aisle. He notices an inscription on the front of the bag: "Riverside Bible Church."

"Sir, we'll need to store that in the back," a flight attendant tells the man. The row of travelers behind him has grown, and irritated stares pierce his back.

"Sorry, I thought it'd fit," he says with an apologetic smile.

The attendant takes the suitcase with her to the back of the plane. She says she will store it there and he will have to wait until all the passengers are off before retrieving it.

"Thank you. I'm really sorry."

The brown-haired man picks up his shoulder bag looks at his ticket stub. He appears confused as Tom stands to let him in, but he slides into the window seat, apologizing again while Tom says nothing.

The man wiggles in his seat, looking out the window and then staring at the row. He clears his throat.

"Um, excuse me?" he says to Tom.

Tom looks at him but says nothing. The last thing he wants is to have a conversation with this man, especially this early into the flight. He knows better than to give passengers next to him an invitation to talk.

"You know, the travel agent told me this was going to be an aisle seat. I guess I should've checked, huh? I don't fly much."

Tom continues to stare at him, saying nothing.

"Would it be a big deal to switch?"

Tom shakes his head, waving his hand and making it clear that's impossible. He looks ahead again.

"Look, I know that might be a lot, but I've been battling a bad stomach thing—I mean, it's not contagious or anything. I just worry—I might need to take a quick trip to the bathroom."

"I can let you out," Tom says.

The man next to him, probably in his early or mid-thirties, wipes the sweat off his temple and smiles a nervous grin.

"I just—I know it's a lot. Maybe just this one time. To be honest, it's been years since I've flown. I'm not the best flyer. And being next to a window kinda freaks me out."

Tom stares at him without making an expression. "You can shut the window cover."

He stares at the seat in front of him while the man next to him continues staring at him, probably surprised at his comment. He slowly stares ahead, and Tom can see him strapping in his belt buckle in silence.

The passengers file by, and the full 767 bustles in the early summer morning. Tom thinks of the last time he flew, and a chill unexpectedly rushes through him.

❖   ❖   ❖

Business travel became a way of life, and making a trip every week became the norm. While working in sales with several different companies, Tom grew used to flying. With Hammett-Korning, he flew less often but still

19

made at least a couple of trips each month. The last flight he took, a red-eye from Dallas to Chicago, ended up being the most turbulent flight he ever rode in.

It's one thing to have turbulence on a normal trip in the daytime. But at night, with darkness blanketing the cabin and only a handful of reading lights on, with the window blinds shut and half the craft empty, massive turbulence is quite another thing. Tom couldn't sleep, and when the turbulence started, it started with a bang. The plane took a hard nosedive and Tom's stomach lurched, just as it would on a roller-coaster ride. It wasn't a quick, two-second drop either, but a lengthy double-digit-second drop. That's what caused the full wave of panic to seep in afterward. He kept imagining the turbulence getting so bad that they would do another nosedive and never come out of it again.

Tom remembers the sick feeling in his stomach, not nausea but a tight, visceral fear. He hadn't felt that way for a long time, and being alone only made things worse. He remembers sitting there in the sanctuary of first class, his palms and the lower part of his back sweating, afraid of dying. And hating the fear, the worthless feeling it gave him. But after half an hour of the worst turbulence Tom ever experienced, the flight became stable again, and Tom ridiculed himself for being so petrified.

"Everyone dies," he reminded himself. His father used to say that a lot. That's why you're not supposed to fear death. And Tom used to believe he didn't fear it. Until that flight.

Now, a couple months later, he scolds himself again for ever giving in to that fear. It's not that he wants to die. There is so much he still wants to do. But dying is nothing to be afraid of. If it's your time to go, so be it.

So be it, Tom hears in his mind as the plane begins to back up. That's what his father always said. He wonders if his father said that the moment his heart seized up many years ago, the seconds before the blood finally stopped flowing and the instant before he died alone on the kitchen floor of their ranch-style home.

When fourteen-year-old Tom discovered the body later that afternoon, he didn't instantly think *So be it.* He wishes he had. And since then he's tried to tell it to himself many times. But deep down, he still feels the same way he felt years ago when shaking his lifeless father's body to try and wake him up.

It's too soon.

He doesn't wish for another father, and he doesn't hold Benjamin Ledger responsible for leaving him. He doesn't long for the kind of backslapping, fishing-buddy kind of father-son love that he's seen in books and movies. He appreciates his Uncle Dale and Aunt Lily, who raised him and his brother. He simply wishes that his father had had more time.

Everyone deserves more time than that.

❖   ❖   ❖

The plane hurtles up into the sky, and Tom realizes he's fine with flying. No fear, just weariness from a long week's worth of work and raw nerves. He hopes to get some rest during this five-hour flight. Perhaps take in the movie they show—enjoy the novelty of being entertained instead of slaving away at a laptop. Perhaps read from the paperback he bought moments earlier in the airport.

Tom ventures a glance at the open window. The man next to him begins to chew on his lips with nervous energy.

"Fly much?" he asks.

Tom nods and stares back ahead.

"I hate leaving the family behind. I'm glad I don't have to do this on a regular basis."

Again, Tom ignores the man next to him.

Moments later, already ten minutes up in the sky, the man next to him reaches into his case and takes out a folder. He begins to read from a stack of papers. Tom is curious but doesn't dare even glance at them. He wants to be left alone.

❖   ❖   ❖

The steady low hiss of air. Muffled conversations between passengers traveling together. The sound of the captain's voice announcing their flying altitude of thirty-six thousand feet and thanking them for flying this airline. The smile of an attractive, uniformed woman in her forties who offers him a drink.

All things normal.

Tom swallows to pop his ears. He drinks his ginger ale and listens to the man beside him work on his sandwich.

"These aren't too bad," the man says, even though Tom's not paying attention to him.

They have been on the plane for almost an hour. The flight attendants have come by and passed out earphones. The movie is an action thriller Tom has never heard of, so he's declined the earphones for now. He'd begun to read the Clancy novel mindlessly when the airline attendants offered lunch. He declined this as well.

Sunlight streaks into the 767. The flight is smooth, allowing Tom almost to forget he is on a plane. His eyes drift shut and he finds himself daydreaming again about his yacht. He pictures himself racing it across the

Pacific, filling it with a dozen of his friends, partying through the night on board his new toy.

Friends?

He'll find them soon enough. People flock toward money. And he'll have enough to buy friends. Companions. Colleagues. Whatever the words might be. He doesn't care. He'll take out his yacht by himself, perhaps with a special friend. Perhaps with that special someone.

That special someone?

His thoughts mock him, so he abandons them. No point in dreaming about the future anyway. The only thing a person can control is the present day, the current moment. Make the most of that, and the rest will follow.

So be it.

He feels no guilt for what he's done. Not even a tinge. Just relief. And a vague wondering if he should feel more than he does.

Tom breathes in the stale airplane air, his eyes shut, his body motionless. He is almost asleep when the explosion reverberates and the plane shakes violently.

Tom's eyes burst open, and he jerks his head to the right where the sound came from. He expects to see half the plane torn away from the blast, but nothing seems different except an odd humming noise from the plane's engines.

Voices can be heard sighing and mumbling. A man in the seat behind Tom curses. The passengers all around stare at one another and continue to look to the right. Several peer out the windows. An airline attendant rushes by.

"What was that?" the man next to Tom asks.

Tom sees the man's knuckles whiten as he grips the armrest.

"I don't know," Tom says. "It didn't sound good."

"It came from the other side of the plane," the man says. "Can you see it?"

Tom looks but can't see over the bodies positioned between him and the row of windows on the other side of the plane. There are three rows of seats in the plane, with the middle section having the most passengers. The faces that glance back at him look drained of color and frightened.

Tom's ears pop.

"It feels like we're going down some," Tom's seat companion says. He looks out his window on the left. "Maybe turning around."

Passengers continue to mumble as one of the airline attendants walks by asking everyone to make sure their seat belts are fastened.

Control, Tom thinks. *Control.*

He balls up his fist as tightly as possible and clenches his stomach against a sick feeling. His ears continue to pop as the plane shifts back and forth.

"Hey, want some gum?" the man next to him asks.

Tom nods and takes a piece.

"Doesn't it seem we've been in this turn for a while?"

His question is a good one. The plane continues to descend, but as it does, they remain in a right turn. There is a continual vibration, a jittery shuddering of the entire plane.

"Folks, this is your captain speaking. It looks like we've had a little problem with one of our engines. We're going to see what we can do, but it looks like we're going to be delayed getting into San Francisco. I'll be giving you some more information, but for now please remain in your seats with your seat belts on."

The captain's tone sounds different from earlier. The autopilot "Good morning and thanks for flying with us" has been replaced with a more grave and honest voice.

"What's that mean—problem with our engines?"

"I don't know," Tom says to the man on his left. "Doesn't seem little to me."

The man rubs his thighs in a nervous gesture as Tom looks past him out the window. He sees the man breathing in and out hard.

"They have more than one engine on these planes," Tom says, worried the man next to him might throw up the sandwich he ate minutes earlier.

"I never travel. Never. They wanted me to go to this West Coast pastors conference, and I figured it'd be fine."

"You a pastor?" Tom asks.

"Yeah. I'm a youth pastor. At a Bible church in Aurora."

Tom nods.

"I'm Kent, by the way," the man says, a worried look on his face. "Kent Marks."

Suddenly, the thought of talking to him doesn't seem as bad as it did minutes ago. It's either that or hearing his thoughts scream at him that the plane is going down. Tom introduces himself.

"Live in Chicago?"

"Wood Grove."

"Up north, right?"

Tom confirms this.

"So you going to California on business?"

"Yes. Actually, I'm moving out there."

"Really?"

"Change of job."

"What do you do?" Kent asks him.

"I work in sales and marketing." Enough said about that, Tom thinks.

An airline attendant in the other row across the plane cabin stops by one of the windows so she can look out at the wing. She studies it for a couple of minutes.

Another attendant walks by, and a gray-haired woman stops her.

"Are we landing?"

"The captain will let you know what is happening," the attendant says, her voice unsure, her body language all wrong. Her face looks tight, pinched, her lips clamping together.

Kent inhales deeply and then swallows.

"You all right?" Tom asks.

"Yeah, I'm fine. Hey, listen, do you have a cell phone?"

"Yes."

"You know, if I have to—you know, make a call—"

"No problem," Tom says, suddenly thinking of the conversation he shared with Janine earlier that morning.

That memory rolls over into thoughts of Allegra. After all this time, he still thinks of her. He can't help it.

What if the plane goes down? What if the pilot comes over the intercom and tells them they have five minutes before a crash landing? He's got a cell phone at his side powered up and ready to go. Who will he call?

Dale and Lily live in Colorado Springs. It's been a while since he has talked with his uncle and aunt, the couple that raised him since he was fourteen. He can call them. But say what?

And then there's Allegra. He's not even sure he has her right number. Maybe she's moved. Maybe she's married. Maybe she's—anything. She could be anywhere as far as Tom knows. It's been years.

Allegra.

The tremor in the plane continues to grow. They continue descending slightly, the airplane still edging to the right. For a moment Tom grabs hold of one of the last memories he ever shared with Allegra. It's a good one. He is a fool to have left her, a fool to have believed the grass would be greener on the other side of a relationship—especially with someone like Allegra. He wanted money and freedom and went for it without looking back, but over the years he has looked back. At this moment, he finds that looking back is one of the only rewarding things he can do.

❖   ❖   ❖

Tom could see the ocean from his bed. The apartment's sliding glass doors were open, and a fresh morning breeze floated in from the balcony. Their bedroom was located on the third floor of the older apartment building, and one of the reasons they rented it was the small deck outside that room. Allegra loved to open its doors and let the seagulls and crashing waves wake them up in the morning.

Slipping on a T-shirt, Tom climbed out of bed and walked out onto the balcony. It was fenced with several wooden beams that were easy to see through.

"About time you woke up!" a voice shouted to him from the sand below.

A caramel-skinned woman with long dreadlocks and surprising green eyes beamed an irresistible smile at him as two surfers walked behind her and checked her out. She wore shorts and a tank top. Tom loved the fact that Allegra never seemed fazed by her beauty or the attention it garnered her. He knew she wanted only one man's gaze on her.

"Whatcha doing?" Tom asked.

"I'm thinking about getting some breakfast."

"Is there still time?"

"If you hurry," Allegra said, her lips curling up with a smile as Tom raced downstairs.

Saturday mornings were always the same. Sleeping in late, waking up, grabbing warm cinnamon rolls and coffee at a beach vendor they knew, getting a blanket and enjoying the breakfast under a sapphire sky, then walking along the beach with coffee, many times hand in hand.

This was their life.

This morning, after they finished their rolls, Tom lay back on the large beach blanket and stared up at the sky. He let out a sigh.

"What?" Allegra asked.

"Nothing. Those were good."

"You stayed late last night."

"I know. I'm sorry."

"Did you have to?"

"Of course," Tom said. "Some people work longer hours than I do."

"You shouldn't have to work that hard."

"I have no choice. It's expensive enough just living in our little closet."

Allegra nudged his shoulder. "It's not a closet."

Tom turned and rested a hand under his head as he stared at Allegra. Her eyes sparkled—sea-green eyes in a golden-sand face.

"How did I get so lucky?" Tom asked.

"What do you mean?"

"To wake up and find myself on the edge of America next to the most beautiful woman in the world."

"Maybe you're still dreaming." Allegra smiled.

"One day I'm going to give you what you deserve."

"What I deserve?" Allegra asked. "What's that mean?"

"A place in the hills. Perhaps down in Newport Beach. A mansion overlooking the ocean."

"That's what we have now."

"What we have now is a beachside apartment. You deserve so much more than this."

Allegra kissed him on the forehead and followed it with a loving beam.

"This is more than I ever wanted."

"What? Our little hole of a place?"

"No. You and I."

Tom bent over and kissed Allegra's arm. "You know, you're the most optimistic person I've met."

"And you're the most kindhearted."

Tom laughed. "Don't tell my coworkers. A kind heart doesn't help sell."

They stood up and walked hand in hand across the cool, wet sand lining the ocean's waves. They talked about the future, about all the things they wanted, about their dreams and desires, about a hundred things that would never happen. Yet both believed for the moment

30

that they could achieve those dreams as long as they walked side by side toward them.

❖   ❖   ❖

The seat jerks as the plane staggers right. Kent finally lets go and throws up into a paper airline bag. Tom feels sorry for the pale, soupy-eyed man who apologizes immediately afterward.

"I'm signaling for an attendant," Tom says as the stinging bite of vomit fills the air.

An airline attendant shows up a couple minutes later, and Tom asks her to take the bag Kent is holding.

"Can you bring him a glass of water?" Tom adds.

Kent clears his throat and sniffs in pain.

"Do you need to use the bathroom?" Tom asks.

"No. I'm fine. Thanks."

The turbulence grows increasingly worse. It's been almost thirty minutes since the explosion, and the 767 has been steadily descending all that time. A few minutes ago, a copilot came back and avoided conversation with anyone as he peered out the windows close to their side of the plane. Then he went to the other side and did the same, vanishing quickly with a solemn look on his face.

Just as Tom is wondering when they'll hear more news, the pilot's steady voice fills the plane with a sickly hush.

"This is Captain Younter with an update on what is happening. It appears that we have a problem with the hydraulic system for the craft. We've decided to land in Glenburn, Nebraska, about a hundred miles northwest of Omaha. Attendants, please initiate emergency procedures."

For the first time in years, Tom actually listens to an attendant talk through the procedures of an emergency landing on the intercom. She announces that the warning "Brace! Brace! Brace!" will signal the passengers to crouch low and hold on to their ankles if possible. As the attendant talks, a young woman behind Tom begins weeping uncontrollably.

"This is pretty severe," Kent says after the attendants are finished.

His eyes still hold tears from throwing up moments ago. Kent takes a sip of his near-empty cup of water.

"Hey, you said you had a phone?"

Tom nods.

"Can I borrow it?"

"Yeah, sure."

Tom listens as Kent dials the numbers.

"Hey, sweetie. It's Daddy." Pause. "I know. I can't wait to see you again. Can you—" Another pause. "I will, I promise. I'll get you something nice. Can you get Mommy on the phone?"

Kent looks at Tom and slowly inhales as he waits for his wife.

"Hey, M. Yeah, I'm still on the flight. I'm borrowing a guy's cell. Look, they're going to have to land the plane somewhere in Nebraska. No, it's okay. There's something wrong with the hydraulics—I don't know what. We've been in a right turn for about half an hour. It's pretty bumpy too."

Tom has the sense he shouldn't be listening, but he has no choice.

"I don't know, M. Just pray, okay? Things will be fine."

Another pause.

"Honey, things will be fine. I promise you. Don't— come on, don't. It's okay. Listen, it will be fine. I just wanted to call—I didn't want to worry you. I just wanted to call."

Tom notices Kent wipes tears away from his eyes.

"M, I love you. Just pray, okay. Things will be fine. We should be landing in a few minutes. I promise I'll call as soon as I'm able to."

Kent nods and listens.

"You too. Bye, sweetie."

Kent snaps shut the phone and gives it back to Tom. "Thanks."

Tom nods, unsure what to say.

"Is there anyone you need to call?"

"No. I'm not married."

"Oh."

"Your wife's name is Emma?"

"No—I call her M for short. Her name is Michelle."

"And children?" Tom asks, knowing the answer but wanting to ask anyway.

"We have two. Britta, who is four years old. She answered the phone." Kent shakes his head and smiles. "She's four going on ten. We have a six-month-old boy, named Eli."

Tom says something that surprises himself. "Do you have any pictures?"

Kent nods, then examines his wallet to produce a few snapshots.

"This is all of us."

Michelle Marks has long, straight blonde hair and a pretty smile. Britta is blonde like her mother and shows a penchant to mug for the camera. Little Eli still has only a few hairs; his wide smile looks like his father's.

"You have a good-looking family," Tom says.

"Thanks."

The plane drops what feels like a hundred feet, and Tom grabs hold of the armrests.

"You ever had this happen before?" Kent asks.

"No. I've been in a few doozies with turbulence, but never an emergency landing."

"They say it's safer to fly than to drive."

"Yeah, I guess that's true. Doesn't comfort me any now."

A moment passes. Tom swallows to pop his ears again. They're beginning to hurt.

"It's Tom, right?" Kent asks.

Tom nods.

"Tom, are you a praying man?"

"Not really."

"Oh. I was just wondering if you wanted to pray with me."

A sudden discomfort seizes Tom. He feels angry for no apparent reason.

"Pray to who?" Tom asks.

"Pray to God."

Tom glances over at Kent and sees the man's earnest face.

"I'm not really into that sort of thing. But you can go

ahead."

"You don't mind me doing it out loud?"

Tom laughs and feels sick to his stomach. "At this point I don't care about anything except making it through this."

"So I take it you're not interested in spiritual things," Kent says.

"Like I said, I don't get into any of that stuff. But I guess I hit the jackpot as far as seats go."

"How so?'

"You're a pastor," Tom replies. "You're a safe bet for surviving a crash. Or praying for some miracle."

This is an attempt at a joke. Neither Kent nor Tom find it particularly funny.

"I don't think it's that simple."

"Probably not."

"Not all prayers are answered, you know."

Tom looks into turquoise eyes. "Is this the point where you start 'witnessing' to me?"

"No. Not if you don't want to hear anything about it."

"Want my take on church?" Tom asks in a cynical tone. "My uncle and aunt went to church all their lives. The same church with the same preacher who spoke about the same things every Sunday. It's a bunch of older people going to hear the same talk every week and then socialize and eat coffee cake and sip coffee and then go home. That's church to me."

"So you went with them?"

"For a while. Then I stopped. The good thing with them—they've never preached at me. I guess they know it wouldn't work."

Kent nods. "What about your parents?"

"Ah yes, my parents. Let's see. My mother left my dad soon after giving birth to me. A real winner he found, huh? Dad died when I was fourteen. He basically believed what I do."

"What's that?"

"You work hard, then you die. That motto."

"And you really believe that?" Kent's voice sounds genuinely surprised.

"That's what I know and see. All this other fantasy stuff—I guess it's nice for people. Like you. Like my aunt and uncle. It makes people feel good. But is it real? I don't think so."

Someone behind them begins to cry again. The longer they descend, the more the plane shakes.

"If you don't mind, I'll pray, okay? I'll pray for both of us."

"Whatever."

Kent closes his eyes and begins to pray. Tom looks at him in fascination, amused at this man's audacity in his beliefs.

"Heavenly Father, I pray for all of us in this plane. I pray for safety in landing, Lord. I pray that, if it be your will, you give us a safe touchdown. I pray for the pilots— that you give them wisdom and strength. I pray for the passengers in this plane, that first and foremost they might know you, whether it is now or even after all this is finished. Lord, thank you for everything you give us—"

The plane bounces and Kent lurches forward, banging his head against the tray table in front of him. He pauses, then continues.

"Thank you for all the blessings you give us. Lord, I pray for my M and Britta and Eli—please keep and protect them. I pray for Tom, Lord. I pray that you open his eyes to your unfailing grace, that you show him the gift of your Son. Give us faith, Lord. And help us through these upcoming moments. In your Son's name, amen."

Kent opens his eyes and finds Tom staring at him.

"Thanks for letting me do that," he says.

"Well, I hope it helps."

The pilot comes over the intercom to interrupt them.

"Folks, this is Captain Younter again. We're about four minutes from touching down. Everyone needs to be in position, with heads down." He clears his throat. "This is probably going to be a rough landing. We're going to do everything we can to get us down safely. If the landing goes as planned, attendants will give you instructions on deplaning."

Passengers all around them have already assumed the crouching position. Tom looks at his traveling companion and takes a deep breath.

"Hope someone hears those prayers of yours," Tom says.

He curls his fists up in a tight ball, wishing this was over and he was on the ground, safe and sound. Before he leans over, he hears the pastor's words clearly.

"You can still pray too. God will hear your prayer."

❖   ❖   ❖

Time passes like an eternity. Seconds cut by, each one incised on his soul. Tom looks down and sees his pair of $350 black shoes. He sees his hands holding his ankles. He looks next to him and sees Kent in the same position, eyes closed and mouth speaking silently.

This is it.

The plane jars and bounces as they continue descending. The speed is unlike any other landing Tom has experienced. It feels as though they're plummeting at full throttle.

Tom thinks of Pastor Kent's last words to him. And with his own mind the only witness, he decides to pray. Why toy around with something like this? He loves his life, or the life that is to come. And now, suddenly, things all feel different. Everything feels different. All he needs is to be on the ground, safe and secure. Then things will be better.

He just needs to live.

"Please—" he starts out.

He doesn't know who to make this prayer out to. The God of his aunt and uncle, the God of the Bible, the God of Pastor Kent? Are all those Gods one and the same? Is there really some deity up above staring down, listening to his prayer?

God will hear your prayer.

"Please, God," Tom silently prays. "Please let me live."

This is his prayer. Tom looks up, and as he does he hears a flight attendant yell, "Get down!" He sees green fields appear and disappear. The plane shifts back and forth, unsteadily.

God will hear your prayer.

This is it. His life might end right now.

Surreal. Everything unbelievably surreal and unexpected.

A baby crying. A baby? On this plane? What will happen to it?

She'll die. Just like I will. Just like all of us will.

Voices mumbling. Weeping. Coughing.

"Brace! Brace yourselves!" the flight attendant yells.

The plane feels like it's flying at takeoff velocity. Even faster. Tom glances up again and sees a cornfield hurtling past them.

And then—

Impact.

❖   ❖   ❖

Flashes pass by.

A bunk bed in a corner.

Dark, haunting eyes of a woman who gave birth to him, a woman he knows only by a few photos unexpectedly found.

A pier on a clear morning.

Handprints on an iced-over car window.

Mahogany wood of an office desk.

Millisecond blasts avalanching in his mind.

A thousand more flicker before him. Tom keeps his eyes open and sees the world catapult on top of itself and hears the sound of held breaths amidst the unconceivable explosion of death he knows he's about to embrace.

The plane floor feels ruptured, jamming up at them. Tom's head bumps forward, and he cuts his lip and tastes blood as his stomach feels lost and spiraling. There is a falling, twirling sensation until just above him a cannon blast roars. Tom hears a crackling, a crushing sound, a breaking and thudding. He suddenly finds himself upside down, tasting black smoke and seeing what he first thinks is the sun but then realizes is the lick of flames all around him. The hurtling movement continues as he feels the entire structure sliding violently ahead. He knows he is going to die.

Then, in a dream, a fast-moving violent music video with only the sounds of crackling and crying and coughing and moaning and screaming, Tom moves and tries to shake off death by charging somewhere to someplace. He unbuckles his seat belt and falls on his head and doesn't even feel the pain as he takes in a breath and feels it burn and tries to see something, anything, but can't. All he sees is a glimmer of light, and can't tell whether it's from outside the plane or from a fire inside it. He rushes toward the light and propels his legs faster and feels his $350 shoes warm up and looks down and sees his feet stepping through fire so he continues to run.

He pushes and jams ahead through voices that shout and scream for help and in pain and that they're going to die. He doesn't hesitate. He expects the plane to explode.

He expects to find himself in a ball of fire. Tom rushes toward the light and soon finds himself falling into a cornfield with stalks bigger than himself.

He coughs violently and then staggers up. The next few minutes or hours—he's lost track of time and place— Tom no longer thinks or feels. He simply reacts. With terror-stricken eyes, he takes in everything around him. He cannot help out. He cannot offer assistance. He feels paralyzed and unsure if he is still alive.

A man tears past him with an arm and his hair on fire.

A body of a young woman is trampled by people exiting the plane.

Tom hears a voice and goes to it in a daze. He hears "Help me." He hears it pleading for him, so he goes back toward the gaping hole in the fuselage he just sprinted out of. He hears the choking screams for help and finds it's the young woman on the ground, her legs all mangled and sticking out in four different directions.

"Help me."

Tom grabs her by the shoulders and slides her away from the mass. He gets her to a group of two other people and lets her go. He begins to walk through the cornfield, then winces and lifts his right foot up. The heel and half the sole of his shoe are gone, presumably burned off. He shakes off the pain and keeps walking through the mass of eight-foot stalks and keeps walking. Smoke wisps between him and the sun. He can't spit out the taste of gas and smoke in his mouth.

He looks back and sees flames and people and four different parts of the plane. He hears sirens and crying and voices.

Tom looks at his hands and sees blood and wonders where he's bleeding. He sits and examines his body and finds nothing wrong except for the cut lip. Most of the blood must belong to the young woman he pulled away from the burning fuselage and left in a cornfield next to the plane. He has no idea if she's even still alive. He stares up at the heavens and doesn't know what to say.

$\diamond$ $\diamond$ $\diamond$

Wake up."

Tom opens his eyes and feels the hand against his cheek. It takes him a moment to see the comforting grin next to him.

"You're here," he says to Allegra.

"Of course I am."

She holds his hand as Tom glances around and finds himself in a hospital.

"How'd you get here so fast?" he asks.

"Don't worry about that. You need to relax."

"I can't believe I made it."

"It was a horrendous crash. Many people died."

"And I lived."

Tom looks at Allegra and finds she looks the same as the last time he saw her. As always, she is dressed impeccably in jeans and boots, with a long, black shirt-jacket over a T-shirt.

"This changes everything," Tom says.

"It does?"

"I'm so sorry. I don't know where to begin. All this time—"

"It's fine," Allegra says.

There is an odd absence of all noise other than Allegra's soft voice.

"Is there still a chance?"

Allegra looks at him and reads his mind.

"No, Tom."

"What?"

"I've come here to say good-bye."

The words sound familiar to Tom. He's heard them before.

"You and I know it's for the best," Allegra says, her voice suddenly becoming softer. "What were we thinking anyway?"

"I don't understand," Tom says.

But he does understand. He understands too well.

"We want different things. I can't keep fooling myself."

"Fooling yourself?" Tom asks, but suddenly he finds that he is talking to himself, that they're not in a hospital, but facing the ocean.

"I'm sorry, Allegra," Tom finds himself saying under a brilliant blue sky.

It's good-bye all over again. Except this already happened once, years ago. And Allegra wasn't the one saying good-bye.

Tom jumps and wakes up and finds himself in the backseat of a sport utility vehicle.

"It's gonna be all right. We'll be gettin' there in just a sec."

A voice he doesn't recognize is speaking from behind the wheel of the fast-moving vehicle.

"Wait," Tom says, exhaling and shaking.

"What's wrong?"

"Please, stop. I'm—I feel sick."

The motion of the SUV is doing this. He feels like his entire body is twirling around and around, the way it might after getting off one of those nauseating amusement park rides.

"Hold on there a sec." He can feel the truck stop at the side of the road, but his body still feels like it's moving.

Tom grabs for a door handle and finds it. He rushes to the side of the road and unleashes the contents of his stomach.

A stranger, an older man, helps him back into the car. Tom lies across the large backseat and lets his eyes close again.

❖   ❖   ❖

Tom finds himself gently nudged awake by the same older man.

"All right there, young fella."

He hasn't been called young fella in a long time. The gray-haired man with long sideburns and teeth in need of major dental work helps Tom out of the vehicle.

"I got it," Tom says, but then admits to himself that he feels a bit woozy.

"We're just gonna make sure everything is okay with you," the grandfather type says to Tom as they enter the hectic lobby of the hospital emergency room.

Tom waits with the older man and watches the scene unfold around him. It seems as though every minute someone new is helped into the hospital, either in a stretcher or a wheelchair or, like Tom, by a stranger's helping arm.

"God-awful, ain't it?" the older man says.

Tom nods.

"I'm Earl. I live about ten minutes away from here, just outside of Glenburn."

"We're in Glenburn?" Tom asks the man, noticing patches of unshaved stubble on his leathery face.

"Yep. Ever been here?"

Tom shakes his head.

"Can I get you anything?"

Tom just wants to be left alone, but in a few minutes he is taken back to an examining room. A red-haired nurse with sympathetic eyes comes in and talks to him like she would talk to a child. She asks if he is okay and asks some basic questions to make sure he doesn't have a concussion.

"You're very fortunate," the nurse tells him. "Leaving something like that with just a cut lip is incredible."

"Is there a way I can check to see if someone's a patient here?" Tom asks.

"We can try, but it might be difficult. Is it a relative?"

"No," he tells her. "Just a guy I was sitting next to on the plane."

The nurse leads him out to the front desk and asks another woman to help Tom. Tom gives her the name Kent Marks, but they don't have anything so far. A man is wheeled past on a stretcher, his head ravaged by burns and his face almost unrecognizable.

Tom turns and begins to walk out.

"Whoa, there. Hey, buddy . . . yeah, you."

The man who brought Tom to the hospital catches up to him and puts a hand on his shoulder. Tom struggles to remember the name. *Earl.*

"We're setting up fort at the college just down the road. For crash victims, I mean. They have a lot of empty dorm rooms 'cause of the summer. There'll be hot food and showers and rooms."

Tom stares at Earl. His head aches, but not because of any injury sustained on the plane. He got out almost without a scratch—just the slight cut on his lip caused by his own teeth.

"I guess I'm not going anywhere," Tom says.

"Probably not anytime soon. You got any family you need to call? Friends?"

Tom shakes his head, then feels his hip to find the palm-sized cell phone still locked to his leather belt. His right hand pats his pants pocket and notes the wallet still there. He hopes the tiny media stick tucked inside is still all right.

My future . . .

"What's your name, son?"

"Tom."

"You need to get some rest—get some food in you and take a nice shower. They have it all set up at Hope College."

"Hope?" Tom asks.

"Yeah, that's the college name. It's a small Christian college."

Tom shrugs and follows Earl out of the hospital. Sunlight beats down on them as Tom tries to remember what day it is.

❖   ❖   ❖

The room awaits a pair of college students ready to

48

be away from mom and dad for another semester. Bare, splotchy tan walls and an empty, open closet square off the one-window room on the second floor of the dorm. A bunk bed occupies one wall of the room, with standard-issue desks and chairs across from it. Tom curls up under the thin blanket someone gave him and feels his body shudder, chilled not from the temperature but from the thoughts that fill his head every time he closes his eyes. Awful thoughts. Sights and smells and sounds that won't go away.

He remembers the baby crying. Wailing. Until it stopped—just like that. He'd forgotten that until now. He wishes he'd forgotten altogether.

There's the glimpse of cornfield again, the world turning somersaults, the bright flames. Then voices in agony. Crackling noises. The smell of spilled fuel and strangling smoke that he can still taste in his mouth.

It is later that night, and Tom wears oversized clothes that must have been donated from a farmer: faded Levis about three sizes too big, held up by his own belt, along with a Glenburn, Nebraska, sweatshirt that reads "burn, Nebra." The chaos at the college when he arrived earlier felt intrusive and bothering—a hundred strangers all wanting to reach out and help someone. There was food in the cafeteria, and preachers were there to pray with people. There were counselors and ordinary citizens simply waiting to see how they could help.

Tom knew he was a victim. He was one of the wounded who needed caring for. But he simply wanted to get away.

A young woman came up to him and gave him a hug

and began to weep. Tom stood there speechless, then finally excused himself without saying a word. He couldn't connect with her tears, and he didn't feel he needed her hugs.

Now, away from the helping people in the sanctuary of his dorm room, Tom turns and wipes the sweat off his brow and begs for sleep.

This is a cell, not an accommodation. And nothing can take away the awful fears inside him.

He thinks about praying, but then feels angry that he had ever prayed in the first place. Sure, he had lived. But what about so many others?

Everyone was speculating earlier that evening in the cafeteria—surmising how many people had lived and how many had died. It was almost a miracle, many said. And Tom supposed his survival might be a miracle. His prayer might have been answered? But that idea simply raised a host of other possibilities he couldn't begin to face. And it didn't begin to stop the terror racing through his mind and heart like a runaway roller coaster.

Everything is so fresh, so raw. He feels his body falling, soaring through the heavens, plummeting to the earth without a parachute to slow him down. The sensation of dropping won't go away.

"Oh, God," he cries out, not sure whether the cry is a plea or a curse.

Tom rarely dreams, rarely finds time for looking back. Sometimes memories spike up and try to splinter his life, but he doesn't allow them to affect him. All his life, especially in his adult years, Tom has found a way to keep the past in the past, to bury himself in his work and set his sights on making a good life for himself. Wallowing in self-pity, like he's doing now, is unusual for him. It is the first time he's felt this way in many years.

He can't seem to shake one thought.

Why me?

Silence crawls over his skin. It whispers evil reminders until his eyes grow heavy and, finally worn down, close.

A jolt awakes him. Tom sucks in air as if it's his first breath after being down in the depths of an ocean. He looks down and sees a seat belt and then glances to the seat on his left. Kent Marks sleeps.

No—

But he's there.

All a dream. An awful, wicked dream.

He looks out the window. They're coasting above billowing, puffy clouds. The brilliant blue of sky makes him squint his eyes.

Tom looks at his hands. Clean. He feels the corner of his lip. Fine. No cut.

Then he looks across the aisle and sees the row of empty seats. His eyes move ahead and sees the same thing in the row ahead, the same thing behind.

He stands up slowly, leaving Kent by himself.

All around him are vacant seats. Empty aisles. Bags and briefcases still visible, table trays still down, clear plastic cups still half full, but not a single soul around.

No one.

He heads toward the back of the massive aircraft and passes row after row of empty seats. He opens the bathroom doors and sees no one. No airline attendants or hyper little children or anyone.

Nothing.

No one.

He breaks into a sprint and passes the unfilled seats on his way to the cockpit. Kent Marks is still in his seat, his slightly open mouth letting out a slight murmur of a snore.

First class is no different from coach. The entire passenger list has vanished.

He pounds on the door to the cockpit and sees it creak open. Inside, he sees empty seats and a control panel all abuzz with blinking signals and whirring gauges.

The heavens open up in front of him through the wide, gaping smile of the cockpit's windows. Tom stares in wonder at the plane flying itself. Then he notices they're not moving forward at all but heading straight downward, hurtling toward a cornfield like a meteor. Racing, blasting toward a tiny stretch of landing field in Nebraska. Dropping toward the ground at an unimaginable velocity, death looming again.

Just before impact, Tom screams and wakes up.

Another boom shakes Tom awake. This time it's not a nightmare but the sound of someone knocking at his dorm room door. Sunlight streaming in the window tells him it's the next morning. He climbs out of the bed's bottom bunk and wanders to the door.

"Good morning," a kid who could easily pass as a college freshman says in a nervous voice. "I'm Ben. I live on campus and—well, we're going around passing out some stuff. Toothbrushes and stuff like that. Some extra clothes."

A plastic milk crate overflows with a variety of items. Tom takes it in his hands and looks at the young man. He has reddish blond hair and acne, and he couldn't weigh more than a hundred pounds.

"I'm sorry about the accident," Ben says. "I'm a few doors down in case you need anything. Room 218. They're serving breakfast in the cafeteria—do you know where that is? Oh, okay. Well, just let me know if you need anything."

Tom nods and says he's not hungry. But thanks.

Ben gives him a formal smile and looks at Tom as though he's a burn victim.

Back in the dorm room, morning sunlight reaches out toward Tom as he sits on the edge of the bed.

How many years ago was college? Tom wonders. *Would I have helped out someone in my shoes?*

He knows the answer to that. In those days, it was always about himself. And it still is, so many years later.

Why is everyone being so friendly, so helpful, so accommodating?

Tom takes a long, scalding shower that eventually turns lukewarm and causes him to climb out in chills.

❖   ❖   ❖

He knocks on the door of 218. The same pimple-faced kid answers and gives him an excited look, as though he is going to finally be able to utilize some of the techniques his psychology class taught.

"Do you have a television?" Tom asks.

Ben tells Tom yes and invites him into the well-lived-in room. Tom instantly hears the whine of the television.

"Have they been showing any footage of it?" Tom asks.

"Yeah. All morning long."

This poster-clad room is bigger than Tom's, with a living room/kitchen area. In one corner is a twenty-six-inch television with clear reception. Ben grabs the remote and starts going through the channels.

"Some guy caught the actual crash on video."

"Doesn't surprise me," Tom says.

"It's unbelievable to look at."

"You should have been inside it."

The kid looks at him, marveling and waiting for Tom to say more. Tom doesn't.

"Here. They've been showing it on here. This is a local station."

A reporter is interviewing grieving family members of one of the victims. Tom watches with a sick feeling inside.

Then they show the footage caught with a local man's video camera. Amateur film work capturing it all.

The screen shows the clear, tranquil sky and the small image of the plane coming down. Then it focuses on the unsteady 767 wavering in the sky, blistering down at an alarming speed. It touches the ground for a second, bounces, then nose-dives and stands on its front like it's doing a handstand. It continues flipping over just as a deathly orange blast erupts in its front section. One wing rips off as the plane completes its eerie cartwheels and finally comes to rest.

Tom thinks of the two-hundred-plus passengers holding on for their lives while the airline attendant screams "Brace! Brace yourselves!"

Tom braced. But so did Kent.

And they were separated by what—inches? A foot or two.

Maybe he's still alive.

Tom knows they probably all should have died. The accident doesn't even look real. Tom can't believe what he's seeing. The impact and the devastation of the landing. The carnage. The absolute *blitzkrieg* of the plane meeting the runway and its surrounding cornfield without proper tools to land.

Photos of the aftermath disturb him even more. The airplane doesn't resemble a long, sleek tube but rather the blackened-out, hollowed-out pieces of some giant toy. The airplane's right wing is reported to have disintegrated immediately, with the remains of the airplane breaking apart as it tumbled down the runway. The center section of the fuselage, which landed in the cornfield, still has its left wing attached. The cockpit separated early and came to rest on the runway, with all the pilots somehow surviving the accident.

Certain words and phrases from the reporters prick Tom. Like *miracle* and *marvel* and *answered prayers*. Tom cannot believe that a plane that turned over on itself and blew up into flames and then broke into huge sections could have had *any* survivors.

The reporter details what they know went wrong. Something about an engine explosion that led to the total loss of all the plane's hydraulics.

Tom ignores Ben's few comments and finally decides he has seen enough.

"Thanks," he tells Ben.

"Do you need anything?" the student asks him.

"Just some air."

A vacant, weathered picnic table sits in the middle of the lines of sidewalks mapping out the college grounds. Tom sits on top of the table. The surrounding maple trees barely allow the sun to warm his dark hair. He watches passing strangers and feels alone.

Tom knows he needs to contact Dale and Lily, his uncle and aunt. They didn't know he was flying. That's a good thing. But sooner or later, someone might wonder. Besides, he needs to see Dale and Lily for his own sake. It's been a long time since he's seen them in person. And regardless of everything going on, he knows it's time to go home.

He thinks of the tiny memory stick still hidden inside his wallet.

A passerby notices him sitting by himself and begins to walk toward him. It's a woman in maybe her seventies or eighties, short and round with a slow walk and cheerful eyes behind thick-rimmed glasses. She reaches the edge of the picnic bench and smiles.

"You're all alone out here," she says.

Tom nods.

"I saw you last night. You're one of the survivors."

The woman speaks without hesitation in a soothing voice, like a mother reading a child a story before going to bed.

"Yes," Tom replies.

"What's your name?"

Tom looks at the woman, her white hair in a bun and her long jeans skirt. The crinkled lines of her face smile at him. Tom rubs a hand through his thick black hair.

"Tom Ledger."

"Did you have any loved ones on that plane?"

"No."

"They say over one hundred people survived the accident," the woman says.

"That means over a hundred died, too."

"You're right," the rich, country-soaked accent says.

"The crash looked awful. Just saw it on the television."

"Dreadful. The fact that anyone lived at all is truly a blessing."

A *blessing*. Tom wants to add up a list of all these nice sayings he keeps hearing.

"Did you know anyone on the plane?" he asks.

"No. I just live in town, came here to offer my services. I'm Gertrude."

Tom greets her with a smile. An honest smile. Normally he would frown at chitchatting with a stranger, but there is nothing normal about this day.

"It's an awful thing. So many families still waiting to hear about their loved ones. They've been arriving all night. There are people here who are missing children, missing spouses."

"You've been helping them?" Tom asks.

"As much as one little old lady can help. Mostly I pray for them and ask if they know the power that Jesus provides."

Another one, he thinks, leery of talking further.

"So can I help *you* out?" the wrinkled smile asks.

"I'm doing okay on my own."

"Do you believe in Christ? In the hope he brings?"

"I'm not sure *what* I believe in anymore," Tom tells Gertrude.

"I'll take that as a no."

"Like I said, I don't know anymore. That's all I want to say about it."

"I think that sometimes people need to go through something awful before they can come to Christ. I had that happen to me. After I lost a child years ago. No one can take the pain away, especially not the world. Yet I know that death for believers is considered a gain."

"What'd you say?" Tom asks.

Gertrude repeats her last statement, and Tom shakes his head and curses.

"What is it?" Gertrude wonders.

"A gain. How could anything like what just happened be a *gain?* That's the stupidest thing I've ever heard in my life."

"I'm sorry if I offended you, Mr. Ledger," Gertrude says. "I will let you be. I just—well, sometimes the Spirit just gets the best of me. But listen, if you need someone to talk to, I'm around."

"Okay."

"It *is* an amazing thing, huh?"

"What?"

"The gift of life. Breathe in and feel it." Gertrude

inhales and closes her eyes. "I'm eighty-seven years old, and I still feel like I can live another twenty or thirty years. Life is such a wonderful thing."

"It's easy to take it for granted," Tom says.

"You have to wonder why things happen, don't you?"

"You believe there are reasons? Like the plane going down?"

"I believe there is a reason for everything, Mr. Ledger. Every big and little thing that happens. I believe in a divine purpose."

"A purpose in people dying?" Tom asks.

"God doesn't want those things to happen. But he allows them to happen."

"You know—it's Gertrude, right? You know what I don't get? People like you always saying there's a reason for bad things that happen. Or that God *allows* them to happen. But I don't get it. If there is such a thing as a God and God is good, why then doesn't he *do* something?"

"But you lived, didn't you? Maybe that's part of what God is doing, part of his divine purpose in that. Have you thought of that?"

"I think I'm just some lucky twit who got out of there alive."

"Maybe so. But I think otherwise. Perhaps one day you will too."

The woman strolls off toward the busyness of the cafeteria, leaving Tom with his thoughts and with the echo of her words.

❖   ❖   ❖

The rush of an eighteen-wheeler blows past Tom as he walks on the edge of a two-lane asphalt road. It is two in the afternoon, and he has been walking for half an hour. Walking to get some air, to find some peace, to figure out what he needs to do. But the walk is making things worse.

He should've already made the delivery last night. Should've already called to let them know about the plane accident. They've surely heard about it. His voice mail had five messages on it, and Tom deleted each one before he finished listening. He is not sure what he will do.

Perhaps they will assume he is dead.

The simmering sun warms him as he walks toward nowhere in particular. The road he strolls beside is busy, with a variety of cars and trucks driving by at speeds of forty and fifty miles an hour. On either side of the road are fields, one populated with cows. There doesn't seem to be much more to Glenburn, Nebraska. Obviously it has an airport and a hospital, but otherwise it's just a little blip on the map.

He wonders once more about Kent Marks, then wonders why he even cares. Part of it is curiosity. He sat right beside him on the plane, so he cannot help but be interested whether the man lived. But Tom knows there's another reason he's interested. If he died, Marks would leave behind a lot of people who loved him. Tom lived, but for what?

A trickle of sweat slowly finds its way down his back. His forehead and nose feel exposed and sunburned. His thoughts still race at a hundred miles a minute, questioning where he should go, wondering what he should do. Should he continue down the path he was on? Has this second chance been given to him for a reason?

But Tom doesn't really believe in second chances. Life is what you make for yourself. Chance is something that happens to those who are too weak to accept the truth about life's realities.

So be it.

Amen.

His head floats in a daze of confusion. Voices, images, sounds—they all combat his sanity. Tom wants them all to leave him alone.

He steps out into the road. He keeps walking until his feet hit the double yellow lines in the middle.

A Ford Explorer driving toward him stalls and edges right, passing him. The car behind it doesn't notice him until it's only ten feet away, when it veers violently to its right and swerves off the road. The driver wails at Tom with his horn and rolls down his window.

"You idiot! What're you doing!"

Tom keeps walking as the man hurls profanity back at him.

A convertible passes from behind, honking. A Honda

Accord slows down as the driver yells "Get off the road!" But Tom still marches down the center line, unfazed by the vehicles and the screaming drivers. He feels oddly unconcerned, strangely absent.

A Camaro races toward him and whips by, missing him by inches. Tom doesn't flinch, doesn't stop, doesn't hesitate. He actually feels good. He can sense the adrenaline flowing through his body, the same way he felt it rush through as the plane went in for its horrific landing.

The sound of a car horn honking from behind him doesn't stop him, either. As the Dodge SUV pulls up beside him, a man rolls down his window. A friendly grandfather with gray hair gives him a puzzled look.

"What are you doin', boy?"

Tom looks up and sees Earl, the man who brought him to the hospital yesterday.

"Just walking," Tom replies.

"In the middle of the road?"

The Dodge continues to inch next to a strolling Tom.

"Good a place as any."

"Tom, right? Come on, Tom. Get in the car."

"I'm fine."

"Tom, please. Come on. You're gonna get yourself killed."

The concept doesn't frighten Tom. Not anymore.

A car drives by and the driver yells at both of them.

"Tom, come on. Someone's gonna feel real awful if they hurt you."

Tom looks into Earl's placid brown eyes and decides to get in. This time he climbs in the front seat.

Earl turns the truck around and heads back to the college.

"You're three miles away from Hope."

"That close?" Tom says. "Feels like I'm a lot farther away than that."

Earl looks at Tom, trying to understand what exactly he means. He lets it go.

"Are you okay?"

"Yeah, I'm fine. Don't worry about me. I just needed to do some thinking."

"Next time just go in a field or something. You're lucky I came by."

"You must be my guardian angel," Tom says.

Earl laughs. "I ain't no angel. Just a local doin' his part. You gotta do your part too."

"What's that?'

"Let people help you."

Tom nods and feels the dampness of his polo shirt as he sits back in the truck.

"I heard the Wal-Mart's gonna open its doors later this evening and let survivors pick up stuff they need."

"I saw that in a game show once."

"This here ain't a game show."

Tom stares at the countryside passing by and doesn't remember walking this far.

"I've got everything I need."

"Do you now?" Earl raises his furry eyebrows and wrinkles his mouth.

"Not you too," Tom begins.

"What?"

"Go ahead. Tell me what you think. Start preaching. Why be any different?"

"Preachin'? What're you talking about?"

"Everybody I've met the last couple of days wants to

save me from eternal damnation. Like it's not enough I just got saved from a plane crash. I've gotta get my soul saved too."

Earl laughs. "Look here, Tom. I'm not about to start talkin' to you about any of that stuff. I'm just a simple man tryin' to help out. Why is that such a problem with you?"

"You don't have any ulterior motives?"

"Hey, I spend most of my time at a bowling alley with a bunch of other guys drinking the days away. My wife died years ago, and my family is spread out all over. I ain't got much of a life. But I know common decency. You help out your fellow man."

"Seems I've talked to some people at the college who are helping out with an agenda."

"What sort?" Earl asks.

"God is great. God is good. Let us thank him for our food."

Earl shakes his head.

"People help out in different ways."

"I don't need those ways."

"But you need to walk down the center of the road? You need to try and kill yourself again? That's the answer for you?"

Tom doesn't say a word to Earl. They drive, and Tom sees a sign pointing to Hope College. Earl ignores it and continues driving.

"Hey, isn't that the—"

"You much of a drinker, Tom?"

Tom shakes his head.

"But you won't be opposed if I buy you a drink or two?"

Tom looks at him and shakes his head again.

"I don't know about you, but I could use one," Earl says.

❖   ❖   ❖

They sit in the bar area of the local bowling alley. Several others sit at the bar, smoking. Neon beer signs line the wall, interspersed with posters advertising beer.

For an hour, Earl tells Tom about his life. Tom notices the change in mood the moment the older man finishes his first Budweiser. Earl's disposition becomes more amiable, more relaxed, and the man becomes more talkative. As Tom works on his own bottle, he remembers why he hates beer so much.

Earl has led a simple life. He is seventy-two years old and has lived alone since his wife, Bernice, died of cancer seven years ago. They have two children, a son who lives about forty minutes away and an estranged daughter who lives in Indiana. Earl doesn't say much about his daughter but acts as though he will never see her again.

Earl worked at the same factory in Glenburn for fifty years, and when Tom asks he says he reckons he liked it. His words haunt Tom. Fifty years. Fifty long years. An entire life lived and breathed and committed to and this man "reckons" he liked it.

Earl sees Tom's amazement at his comment.

"And you? Do you love what you do?"

Tom laughs. "Haven't for a while. I just quit my job."

"When?"

"Yesterday."

"Timin's interesting."

"Sales and marketing. Two crocks if I've ever heard of any."

"How so?"

"You ever been in sales?"

"Can't say that I have," Earl says. By now he's halfway through his second beer.

"Everything is bottom line. Everything is how many products you move. It doesn't matter if you're selling horse heads; you have to move product. You build relationships with clients you despise and work all sorts of hideous hours and travel everywhere just to try to sell those horse heads."

"You sell horse heads?" Earl asks with a furrowed brow.

"Of course not. But I might as well have. You sell one thing, you sell anything."

"So you just quit sales."

"I went from sales to marketing. Promotions, you know. Moving up a corporate ladder. It's all politics. A guy I know started sleeping with this woman veepee, and the next thing you know he got promoted."

Earl snorts. "Sounds like one of those soap operas the wife used to watch."

Tom laughs. "That's nothing. The stories I could tell."

"I'm listenin'."

"For years, I had a boss who said he was going to fire me every week. Seriously. He told me if my sales numbers weren't high enough, he'd fire me. Did it just to intimidate me, you know? For a while, my numbers weren't very good, but this guy was just blowing hot air. I turned out to be the company's best salesman and eventually became *his* boss."

"What company you work for?"

"Doesn't matter," Tom replies.

"And this fella, what happened to him?"

"The first week he reported to me, I told him I was going to fire him if he didn't meet my expectations. Then the next week came, and he came into my office with lousy numbers and a smug smile on his face. I told him there was a difference between him and me. When I say something, I mean it."

"So you fired him?"

"Yep. Just like that."

"Wow."

"Yeah, but I've always been one of the good guys. I know veepees on drugs. These really rich guys who have different girlfriends in different cities around the country. One lady who was blackmailing her way to the top."

"And all that sort of stuff really happens?" Earl asks.

"Yeah. Corporate politics can be awful. It depends on what company you work for."

"Still sounds more exciting than the factory."

"Did you hate the people you worked around?"

"Nah," Earl says. "I had some good buddies working there."

"I never really knew the people working around me. They were like people riding with you in an elevator. You're stuck with them. But you know you're eventually going to get off the elevator and on to other things, so you don't invest much time and energy in them."

"That's what you think about people?" Earl asks, working his third beer now.

Tom reflects for a second. "I was talking about work."

"And what about home life? Family? I find it interestin' that after you almost lose your life there's no one you need to contact. No one you need to see."

"Says who?" Tom asks.

"Well, you're sittin' in a bowling alley bar with an old man you don't know. I might be country and a bit worn around the edges, but I can see what's plain in sight."

"I'm thinking about going to see my aunt and uncle. They basically raised me."

"That's good," Earl says. "Any other family? Wife? Ex-wife? Children?"

"I've got a younger brother who was living in Arizona the last I heard. No one else."

"So these people, these coworkers of yours—these elevator people. If your family is all gone and you work all the time, who do you consider your friends?"

Tom shrugs. "I told you, I quit."

"But quit to do what? I remember when I retired, I had a list of about a hundred things I wanted to do."

"Have you done them?"

"Nah, not really. A lot of them involved Bernice, and she's gone. But I still got my friends and such. Life's not worth living if you live it alone."

Tom finishes his beer. "Thanks for the Bud."

"Want another?" Earl asks.

"No. But I'm guessing you might."

"Maybe one more before we hit the road."

"Should I drive?" Tom asks.

Earl laughs out loud. "You kiddin' me? I'd be crazy

71

letting you drive. No, I'll do the drivin', thank you very much. Safer that way."

Tom stands in a line for the buffet set in the kitchen of the cafeteria. The food selection is immense, with chicken and ham and steak and more than a dozen side dishes to choose from. Tom isn't hungry, but he knows the food will do him good. He takes a chicken breast and some mashed potatoes, then looks for a seat.

Earl dropped him off over an hour ago. It's around seven in the evening, and the dimly lit cafeteria looks like a town hall meeting, filled with people talking and eating at round tables for eight. Tom wishes to be left alone, so he takes his plate to an empty table.

Ten minutes later, he spots the man for the first time. The well-built man in khaki slacks and a white polo shirt appears uninterested in having dinner. His narrow eyes scan the room the moment after he enters. Tom takes a bite of chicken and keeps his eyes on the stranger. The man finds Tom and then walks toward his table, his eyes unblinking and his mouth tightly shut.

"Tom Ledger?" the throaty bass voice asks.

"Yeah?" Tom says, glancing around to see if anyone is watching them.

The man slides out a chair and fills it next to Tom.

His face under the dark crew cut looks freshly shaved and remarkably flawless except for one mole on his left cheek. His jawline is pronounced when he doesn't talk.

"Mr. Sloan asked me to come get you."

Tom looks back at the door, then again at his unexpected dinner guest.

"That was quick."

"He has requested that you come with me," he says.

"Really?"

"It would be best."

Sliding his fork on his half-finished plate and downing the rest of his iced tea, Tom glares at the man across from him.

"Does Mr. Sloan know about the accident?"

"Yes."

"Maybe I'm not ready to leave."

"It would be in your best interest to come with me."

Anger tears through Tom. He should have known this was coming. He shouldn't be surprised. But he is anyway.

"Why don't you tell him that I almost *died* yesterday. And that I'm waiting to hear about a passenger. Okay? I'm not ready to go anywhere."

"He said you could have another night here, but tomorrow we must leave."

"And I have to go with you?" Tom asks.

"I have a Town Car ready. It will be comfortable."

Tom notes the man's thick forearms and wonders what other things this man does besides drive a car for Mr. Sloan.

"Give me till tomorrow."

"The morning, then," the man says.

"Yeah."

"Mr. Sloan would like to know about the safety of the package."

"Tell him everything's fine, and that I appreciate his interest in my well-being."

The man stands up and strides away. Tom stares down at the rest of his dinner and feels slightly nauseous.

He walks over to a table in the corner that's been designated as Information Assistance. The blonde woman behind the table beams a charitable smile at him.

"Can I help you?"

"Yeah. I'm wondering about the passenger list—I'm trying to get information on someone who was on the plane."

"Are you family, sir?" the sweet voice asks.

"No. I, uh, was sitting next to him. His name is Kent Marks."

"And your name, sir?"

"It's Tom Ledger."

The woman's face tightens as she leafs through a file folder containing pages of documents. She studies one page for a moment, then looks up at Tom with a sad glance.

"I'm sorry, sir. They have him listed as deceased."

Tom nods. *Just as I thought.*

"Are you okay, sir? We have people here who might be able to be of assistance."

"No. Do you know—what are the procedures for family members?"

"The airline has already contacted them personally. We have staff who are here to counsel family and friends of those lost."

She sounds as though she's said this before. Many times before.

"Thanks. I was just—just curious."

Tom walks out of the cafeteria and into the fading light of dusk. Once again he's forgotten what day it is. He strides down the sidewalk, passing strangers holding one another and greeting him with sympathetic glances. Their faces seem to commiserate with his own darkly shadowed one, saying, *"We understand what you're going through and we feel your pain."* Yet Tom cannot relate to them. He has lost nothing. He has no right to feel sorrow or loss. The only thing he lost was some luggage and a bit of his cockiness.

Tom sits on a stone bench and stares at the sidewalk. Then he notices a sign at the fork in the sidewalk that reads,

HOPE COLLEGE
←South Hall   West Hall →

He shakes his head over the college logo at the top of the sign. It bears the image of a cross inside a shield.

The sky with its thin sheet of auburn-soaked clouds reaches out toward an infinite horizon. Tom gazes up and marvels not just at this majestic sight, but at the fact that he has gone so many years without appreciating a single sunset.

T om awakes with a surge of fear.

Pitch black drowns him, but it's not the dark he's afraid of. He looks at the glowing dials of his Mulvari watch—more expensive than any Rolex, yet surprisingly simple in design with its leather band. It's three in the morning.

He slips into some donated jeans and a T-shirt and makes sure he has the few possessions that he carried into this room. He brushes his teeth in darkness and then quietly opens the dorm-room door.

The hall is brightly lit. Tom looks both ways and then quickly strides toward the exit sign at one end. He makes it down one set of stairs and finds the lounge room he located earlier. The window is as he left it, with the screen off in a corner and the window already nudged open. He pulls it all the way up and then slips out to the grass behind the dorm.

He sprints across the large, open field behind the dorm. He is glad to be wearing tennis shoes, even if they are a size too small. He knows that someone is probably watching the front door of the dorm, maybe the same man who approached him at dinner.

He reaches a thick stand of trees and is reminded of two nights earlier, when he slipped through the woods next to the Hammett-Korning office building.

Everything's changed.

Part of him thinks that it hasn't, that everything can still go as planned. All he needs to do is wait for morning, to get in the waiting car and be taken to Mr. Sloan and the others awaiting his package.

Tom can't really explain why he's not going to do that. But earlier this evening, right around the time he was sitting on that bench looking at a college sign and thinking about the sunset, he made his decision. He is not going to carry out this plan of his. Not anymore. Not the way it was going to happen.

The consequences of that decision—he can deal with those later. Part of him doesn't even care about them. The last thing he wants is to get on with his life as though nothing happened.

Something did happen. Something big happened. And somehow, something has to change.

There are more important things now he must attend to. Going to see a man he's met once in his life and made a deal with, an unwise and greedy deal that was probably always too good to be true, is not at the top of his list.

Tom finds the dirt road he is looking for. As he begins to walk down it, a pair of car lights blasts through the darkness and illuminates the entire road for half a mile down. Tom looks back at the trees, ready to run for cover if necessary. He squints his eyes as the vehicle races toward him.

The vehicle soon is next to Tom, and a now-familiar voice tells him to get inside.

Tom walks around Earl's SUV and climbs inside for the third time in the last couple of days. They drive down the street and away from Hope College.

❖   ❖   ❖

"You got everything you need?" Earl asks Tom as they sit in the parking lot next to a closed supermarket.

Tom nods. "Look, I don't have much money on me now, but if you just let me—"

"I don't need any money. What do I need money for?"

"The bowling alley?" Tom asks, trying to make a joke.

"I got enough for that. Listen, it's not a problem."

"Thanks for understanding. For setting all of this up without asking for an explanation."

"It's your credit-card bill. I'm not responsible for the rental car."

"Thanks for getting it for me, though."

"I got you a pretty good one. Sorta fits you. A red Ford Mustang. Convertible, too."

Tom chuckles. "Earl, what can I say?"

"Say you'll let me know how all this pans out."

"All right. I will. I promise."

"You know where you're headin'?" Earl asks.

"Toward Colorado Springs. That's where my aunt and uncle live."

"Won't take you that long, starting early like this."

"Thanks for all your help. I mean, taking me to the hospital and rescuing me off the road and all."

Earl nods, then hands Tom a plastic bag weighed down by something heavy.

"What's this?" Tom asks.

"Ah, just a couple of things. Some bottled water, some snacks in case you need something in the car. And . . . a little something I found at home and don't have much use for."

Tom pulls out a five-by-seven leather book that appears worn out.

"It belonged to my wife," Earl says. "It was her Bible."

"I can't take this."

"No, please. I want you to."

"Earl, I told you, I'm not into this—"

"And I told you that I'm not, either. Look. My wife swore by it. She always used to read stuff to me. It's not like it's a book on witchcraft or anything. It's got some good things in it, I reckon. I just—you probably need it just as much as I do. And you're younger."

"What's that supposed to mean?" Tom asks.

"You get to be an old man, you get set in your ways. I came by my beliefs and convictions years ago, Tom. But you—you're still a young kid. You got a lotta livin' left to do. And for some reason, you made it outta that crash. Maybe there is a God lookin' out for you."

"Don't you go and start preaching at me like every- one else I've met," Tom says, putting the Bible back into the bag.

Earl laughs. "Wouldn't know what to say if I started. Look—just keep the Bible. Read it if you're bored or need some answers. Or call me—I'll give you a few of my own."

Tom shakes Earl's bony hand. "I promise I'll call. Thank you for everything."

"Take care of yourself. And return that rental car in one piece. Bobby did me a big favor leaving it out here like this, and I don't wanna get in trouble."

Tom gets out into the cool night and nods good-bye to Earl.

❖   ❖   ❖

The Mustang glides fluidly down Interstate 80 at eighty-five miles an hour as it approaches the border of Nebraska and Colorado. The top is down and, thanks to Earl, Tom is wearing sunglasses that look to be worth about five dollars but do the job nevertheless. Tom has been driving for six hours, minus a stop at McDonald's for breakfast. The stretch of highway and the open sky with its long blasts of whipped-cream clouds invigorate Tom. This morning things feel different. Everything feels—what? New? Fresh? Vibrant and real?

Alive. That's it.

Tom feels alive. Everything feels alive. Never before has Tom consciously thought of his existence and appreciated simply breathing in and out. The wind rushing at him, whipping his hair and his shirt. The sun bearing down on his forehead and cheeks. The countryside of rolling fields with their lush greens and browns. The blast of the music stations he constantly changes. Everything sounds good to him: the wail of a pop diva, the twang of a country ballad, or the blare of a rock song.

He switches the radio channel during a commercial break and finds a familiar drum-machine intro. Hearing

Phil Collins begin to croon "Take Me Home" is enough to carry him back to the summer of 1985, when the song was so popular.

That was the summer after he graduated from high school, back when the future stretched wide open in front of him like the highway he's driving on now. He had the grades, the abilities, the *drive* to do anything he wanted. He'd been accepted at his college of choice, the University of Southern California, and couldn't wait to leave his little world of Colorado Springs. He longed to experience bigger cities and bigger opportunities—a bigger *life,* full of travel and adventure and romance and the wealth and success he knew he would achieve. He was eighteen, and the whole world seemed new and fresh and alive.

Now he's going back home, going back to the place he dearly wanted to leave, the place where his uncle and aunt live out their daily existences with little expectation of seeing or even hearing from him. It has been a year and a half since he last saw them, and that was during an obligatory Christmas visit. The last time he spoke to them was when Aunt Lily actually caught him at work several weeks ago and managed to get fifteen minutes of the standard "Life is well" out of him.

Overlooked and underappreciated, his uncle and aunt are the two people Tom knows he needs to go see first. Not for their sake, but for his.

The bag next to him flaps, and Tom sees the Bible inside with its fluttering pages opening and closing. He looks past it and grabs one of the bottled waters, opening it and downing a quarter of the warm but satisfying drink.

He still can't get over how readily Earl agreed to pick him up and arrange for a waiting rental car. Tom simply said he was in a bit of a bind and needed to see his uncle and aunt as soon as possible. Tom made it clear to Earl that someone else was waiting for him and that his departure needed to be as clandestine as possible. Earl helped him out far more than Tom ever expected.

I would have never done something like that, Tom thinks.

Now, everything seems different. Before the accident, he was in no rush to see Dale and Lily. Before, he avoided talking about his little, lost brother, and he worked hard to keep all thoughts of Allegra in the distant past, where they belonged.

Before. He thinks of the word he just used. *Before.* Meaning that he's living now in the *after* world. After the accident. After nearly losing his life. Has he changed? Have things truly changed for him?

He thinks again of the pastor who sat next to him in the plane and of the words the man spoke in those last few minutes before the crash.

"I pray for Tom, Lord. I pray that you open his eyes to your unfailing grace, that you show him the gift of your Son."

Kent prayed for him. Tom had forgotten about that. The pastor who prayed out loud actually prayed for him specifically.

Tom still does not understand the meaning behind his words. Unfailing grace? Gift of your Son? Tom tended to view such phrases as nothing but feel-good Christianese. But coming from the earnest pastor, did they really mean more?

He prayed for his own safety and died. How's that for a prayer?

Still, remembering the prayer bothers Tom. At the time, he assumed Kent's prayer was all for naught, that it went unheard because there was no one to hear it. He still believes this, in fact, but somehow the conviction feels less intense than usual. Somewhere at the edge of his mind is a tinge of doubt. A wondering.

Could there really be such a thing as God and an afterlife?

Questions for the ages. Questions Tom always believed he knew the answers for and rarely bothered to ponder.

Now he asks them again and this time doesn't say an absolute, guaranteed no. Something in him leaves room for the possibility, even completely remote and minute, but still . . .

Tom glances in the rearview mirror and sees a car speed up behind him and then remain close behind the Mustang's bumper. It's the third time this morning he's seen the menacing grille of the black Lincoln Town Car, but it was never this close. Nothing but a pair of sunglasses can be seen behind the Town Car's steering wheel.

He slows the Mustang down to seventy-five, then sixty-five, then fifty miles per hour. The car behind him slows to the same pace and keeps close to his rear bumper.

The man Sloan sent, Tom's mind shouts.

That's enough of a realization to allow Tom to floor the gas pedal and speed away. The faster he races the car, the harder the wind whips in his face. The hulking machine behind him accelerates at the same speed, keeping behind him.

The four-lane freeway points straight ahead, with a grassy median strip separating the two westbound lanes from the oncoming traffic. The Mustang veers past one car in the right lane, then another in the left lane, as it hurtles past ninety miles per hour. The pursuing Lincoln stalks him, having no problem keeping up with him.

Yellow lines on the highway rocket past Tom like tracers in the night. He holds the steering wheel in both hands and continues to propel the Mustang as fast as it can go. He sees an eighteen-wheeler ahead beginning to pass another, slower moving car, yet he doesn't hold off on the pedal. Instead, he stays in the right lane and then passes the slow-moving car on the narrow shoulder, shooting up dirt and rocks as the right tires spit up the ground. The Town Car slows down a bit and does the same.

Tom gets back in the open highway and races toward the nearest exit with a small lag time between him and the chasing car. He's not really sure what Sloan's goon would do if he simply stopped the car and climbed out and asked what the problem was. Does the man have a gun? Thinking back on the time he met with Sloan and his men, Tom assumes he's armed. He also assumes this is not a man to disregard.

An exit sign shows a lane veering off to the right of the highway. At seventy miles an hour, Tom takes the exit and finds the car scraping against a metal beam meant to keep people like himself on the road. He jams on the brakes as he approaches the stop sign but he doesn't actually stop. Instead he skids through the intersection, turning right, and heads toward the gas station on the opposite corner.

Tom turns in and then swerves around to face the road, slightly hidden behind a fueling island. He feels his heart thumping hard and takes a quick breath.

So much for the enjoyable summer drive, Tom thinks.

He keeps a foot just above the gas pedal in case he needs to peel out. He watches the road, and, sure enough, the sleek and shiny dark car finds its way toward the gas station. Tom curses and hopes the car doesn't see him.

The Town Car pulls into the station and stops at the entrance. Tom realizes he will have to pass in front of the Lincoln in order to get back onto the side street. He hesitates and sees the idling Lincoln just waiting, as though it knows Tom is there and is simply daring him to do something.

Tom jams on the gas and heads toward the edge of the gas station where an air pump and a pay phone stand. He slows down a bit, then drives over the large, concrete curb with the two front tires of the Ford. His car clunks down, and there is a violent scraping noise underneath the car as he drives over the barrier. The back tires raise the car up for a second, then they slam back down and he's driving over grass. He spins the tires as the car swerves back onto the street and toward the highway.

In his mirror, Tom can see the Town Car turning around.

He races past a plodding Honda Civic with a hunched-over man who tries to glare at him but isn't quick enough. The Mustang takes the sloping curve at another frightening speed as Tom steers it toward the highway. He figures he's given himself another few seconds on the Town Car.

The entrance ramp merges into a lane on the interstate, and Tom cuts off a car in the process. He moves ahead, ignoring the indignant sound of a honking horn.

No one in front of him. Just two straight, open lanes that go on for miles.

The speedometer inches up. Past 100. Then 120. Then as far as it can go.

Tom feels the car shaking a bit and knows that any sudden jerk would send it careening across the Nebraska interstate. The steering wheel jitters, and the wind stings his face. His sunglasses blow off and he has to squint to see the road before him. The Mustang passes one truck, another car, several exits. Interstate 80 merges into Interstate 76 and the border for Colorado approaches. Tom flies by it as fast as the car can go.

After a few more minutes of racing like this, worried more now about a cop pulling him over than the chasing car, Tom slows down to a more reasonable speed of eighty-five miles an hour and finds the closest exit. He is soon driving down a side road and decides to continue to do so for a while, heading south on a winding two-lane blacktop. He drives this way for an hour and finally figures he is far enough away from the Town Car to stop. Tom finds a small diner and parks behind it, then decides to grab some lunch.

Out of his car, Tom stretches and feels the wave of adrenaline pass. He looks at the sign that reads American Grill and figures he's far enough away from civilization to be safe. For the time being, anyway.

❖   ❖   ❖

The smell of bacon and eggs inspires Tom to order breakfast even though it's past noon. The restaurant is small, with a half-wall separating the dining room from the kitchen. He sits down at a square table with places for four and looks around. He's in a room full of what looks to be the regular crowd—folk who know each other well and sit close together, conversing amongst themselves and joking with the waitress, who knows them all by name. It takes five minutes before her grin subsides and she comes over to ask Tom what he wants.

He asks for a Coke and asks the beanpole of a waitress for some more time on deciding what to order. As he looks over a menu, Tom sees a busboy walk past him carrying a plastic tub. He's really not a boy at all, but a Hispanic man in his forties, and Tom notices that he keeps his head and eyes aimed at the floor as he walks. He starts to clear a nearby table, and Tom catches a glimpse of the massive scar on the right side of the man's face. At first Tom thinks it might be a birthmark or some kind of skin discoloration, but a further glance confirms that the skin has been damaged in a fire. The scar is tight and thick in texture. It looks like the man is wearing a mask over half his face. Tom finds himself gawking, then turns his eyes back to the menu.

The busboy wipes the table down and takes away the dishes he cleared. He keeps his head down as he moves past Tom and the crowd of lunchgoers.

All of a sudden, Tom has a strange thought.

Wonder what kind of life he's had.

He feels something unfamiliar ripple inside him—a sort of sympathy for this man. Stuck in the middle of nowhere, clearing tables, bearing an unconcealable scar on his face. What kind of life would that be?

Tom orders an omelet and bacon and eats the food as quickly as it is served. The lunch crowd of eight or nine people dwindles down until Tom is the only one left in the restaurant. The busboy with the scar on his face comes back around to clear off the tables. Tom catches himself staring at the man again.

"How are you today?" a deep Latino accent asks in a friendly, service-oriented way.

"Good, thanks," Tom says.

As Tom goes to pay the check a few minutes later, he looks around to find he's alone with the straw-haired, skinny waitress.

"Could I ask you a question?" he starts.

"Yeah, sure."

"The guy who's busing the tables—you know, the one with the—"

Tom points his finger along the side of his face.

"Yeah. Pedro."

"What happened to him?" Tom finds his blunt question out of character.

"His apartment building in Denver burned down while he was in it. Almost died. His arms and hands got pretty messed up, along with half of his face. He says he should've been killed, but he got a second chance."

Tom nods, intrigued by this tale.

"He is one of the nicest guys I've ever met. Bighearted. Great sense of humor."

Tom nods. Before leaving, he gives the waitress a twenty and tells her to keep the nine-dollar tip. She thanks him and disappears into the kitchen. A minute later Pedro comes out and nods at Tom as he clears off the last table.

A second chance.

Tom wants to ask Pedro about that. What's a second chance like, and what do you do with it? Does it suddenly change you? And if you're not changed, does that make you an evil person?

"Gracias," Tom says to Pedro as he stands. The man smiles and nods good-bye to him.

Outside, Tom squints and finds his waiting convertible gleaming in the sun. The leather seats have been baking in the midday heat, and Tom has to sit down gingerly. He starts up the car and finds both his hands shaking as they grip the steering wheel.

The two-story, two-thousand-square-foot house resembles a log cabin tucked away on the edge of a mountaintop. Located in the Black Forest area about twenty minutes north of downtown Colorado Springs, this is Uncle Dale and Aunt Lily's retirement home, the place they planned and saved for and built after Tom and his brother moved away. Tom can count on one hand the number of times he has stepped onto this particular porch and knocked on the door.

Tom and Sean are the only children Dale and Lily can claim as their own. Tom's father, Benjamin Ledger, was the oldest of three siblings, and Lily was the youngest. After that fateful day when fourteen-year-old Tom found Benjamin dead, Dale and Lily never even hesitated about taking in the two boys.

They were conscientious parents to both Tom and Sean, working hard to impart rules and a worldview without being dominating or critical—a difficult task with half-grown boys who had never had either. More important, Dale and Lily also loved them, and their love showed.

For many years, Tom didn't know or necessarily care

why Dale and Lily never had children of their own. Only years after Tom graduated from high school and went off to college did he learn that Lily could never have children of her own and that Dale and Lily had decided a long time ago against adoption. In some ways, having Tom and Sean enter their lives was an answer to their unceasing prayer for a family.

Tom remembers how angry he felt when he heard Lily say this, how he sputtered when he asked how his father's death could be an answer to prayer. He also remembers Lily's stricken look as she realized how her comment had hurt him. She apologized profusely. But she also said she believed God often allows wonderful things to happen in the midst of tragedy. Tom simply replied that a God who would kill off someone's dad to help another couple out wasn't a God for him.

Back now after such a long time, Tom knocks again and then decides to open the door. Unlocked, of course. He steps onto the dark wood flooring, enjoying the warm, woodsy feel of the spacious entryway. A small bench stands near the door with a variety of antique items sitting on it. An antique musket hangs on one wall and a real moose head greets newcomers on another. Tom knows this is not an animal Uncle Dale has killed. Neither Dale nor Lily has the heart to kill anything, nor the bravery to stand in front of a four-hundred-pound beast and shoot it dead. The moose head, along with several other hanging animals, came from a shop. It simply adds to the look and feel of their own personal mountain lodge.

"Hello?" Tom says out loud.

It's six-thirty in the evening, and Tom assumes it's dinnertime. No one responds to his call, yet he believes both his aunt and uncle are home. He saw Dale's flatbed pickup in the driveway, parked in front of the garage. Lily's Cadillac is probably inside, polished and spit clean.

The scent of barbecue gives them away. Tom walks toward the open kitchen and family room and spots his aunt and uncle on the deck behind the house.

He opens the door and sees his aunt's shocked expression turn into one of utter delight.

"Tom!" she says.

Aunt Lily, a broad, gray-haired woman whose face shows every emotion, rushes over to Tom and smothers him with a hug.

"What are you doing here?" she asks.

Uncle Dale stands behind the grill, his lean physique humorously contrasting with the four hefty chicken breasts he's smothering with sauce.

"I figured this would be the only place I could come for good barbecued chicken," Tom replies as he walks toward his uncle and shakes his hand.

"Just in time," Dale replies, his bald head peppered with sweat from standing behind the blazing gas grill.

"Still using your homemade sauce?" Tom asks.

"Wouldn't use anything else."

Aunt Lily wants an answer. She stands looking at Tom with utter amazement and glee . . . and a hint of suspicion.

"Is everything okay?"

Tom nods. The whole trip, he has wondered what he will say to them. Does he start in on the plane crash? Does he avoid that subject altogether? Does he mention anything about the pastor next to him, about all the questions that fill his mind?

And then there is the matter of Sloan. He's bound to send someone to his uncle and aunt's place as soon as he discovers who they are. And Tom has no doubt he will discover it.

"Yeah, things are fine," Tom says.

"Then, what are you doing here? Is it Sean? Is Sean okay?"

Tom shrugs. "Last time I heard from him, he was."

"When was that?"

"A month ago. Maybe more."

"Well, I just spoke with him last week, and he's fine—"

Tom places an arm around his aunt's shoulders. "I just happened to be in Colorado Springs. Wasn't sure I was going to be, but it worked out that way. Didn't want to tell you guys and then have to renege."

"Like you always do," Lily's tone was light, but her round face showed her disappointment.

"I know. I was wondering—you guys mind if I stay here for a few days?"

Dale's eyes send his wife a surprised look, one of those reading-the-mind glances where a husband and a wife share something unnoticed by most everyone else. Tom knows them, however. He's family and he's not stupid.

"I know—it's been a long time," he tells them. "I'm not going to bail this time. Not like last time."

"Are you sure everything is okay?"

Tom nods, fighting for control of his emotions. All of a sudden he feels a profound sadness seep inside of him, and he has no idea why.

"Yeah. I'm alive, right?"

He laughs as his aunt replaces her concern with an

95

accepting smile and then goes inside to get another place setting. Talk with Uncle Dale about the house and retired life and barbecue sauces begins. Tom looks at the cooking chicken breasts and the flickering flames beneath them. He finds it hard to believe that it's only been a couple of days since he found himself surrounded by char-black smoke and fire and death.

Since he somehow managed to rush to the light and escape with his life.

❖ ❖ ❖

"So tell us what's been going on with you?"

Tom sits back on the plush white couch that would be terribly impractical for anyone with children or pets. He takes a sip of his iced tea and remembers how much he loves Lily's sweet tea. He looks at his uncle and smiles.

"I quit my job a few days ago."

Could that have only been a few days ago? Tom's mind asks. It feels more like a year ago, a lifetime ago.

"Tom—" his aunt says in surprise.

"It's fine. I needed to. I needed a fresh break."

To do what?

"Do you have something else in mind? Something else lined up?"

Tom shakes his head and sees the concerned wrinkles on Aunt Lily's face. Dale's nonchalant expression doesn't change, but then it rarely does. His dark blue eyes look at Tom with curiosity.

"Do you want to stay in marketing?"

Tom still finds himself unsure about what he's going

to say next. Part of him, for some reason, wants to keep the last few days to himself. He's not sure why he can't open up and tell his uncle and aunt—basically, his parents—what happened. But it's been two and a half hours since he's greeted them and he's been unable to get himself to tell them about the crash.

He clears his throat. "Look, there's something that happened the other day."

"What?" Lily asks. She's a pessimist by nature and assumes the worse. With two boys like Tom and Sean to worry about, Tom understands why.

"I left Chicago the other day and was heading toward San Francisco."

His uncle and aunt don't react.

"On Tuesday. On National Flight 2171."

Lily raises her hands to her face, and her eyes bulge in horror. "Tom—"

"You were on that flight?" Dale asks.

"I was on the plane, the one that went down."

Lily goes over to sit beside Tom, holding his arm.

"It's okay," he tells her. "I'm here. I'm fine."

"Were you with anyone—did you have any—?"

"No, I was alone." Tom lets out a sigh, relieved to have told someone.

"I, well, basically got out without a scratch." His hand moves up of its own accord to finger the small cut on his lip. "Well, almost without a scratch."

"Why didn't you call?" Lily's eyes well up with tears.

"I didn't want you to worry," Tom says, holding her hand. "I don't ever want you worrying."

"I can't believe it."

"What was it like?" Dale asks. "On the plane, I

97

mean."

"We all knew something was up when the explosion occurred. Something about the hydraulics."

"I saw it on the news. They're saying that it was a complete hydraulic failure. The pilots couldn't control the plane."

"Yeah. We were in a right-hand turn and kept in one for almost forty minutes or so."

"The news said it was a miracle that anyone survived at all," Dale says.

"Was it terrifying?" Lily says, still holding on to him.

"Yeah, it was pretty bad. But I made it through."

"You should have called. We would have come for you."

"But there was nothing you could do. I was all right."

"From what I heard, a lot of people made it through all right," Dale says. "Amazing that anyone would survive something like that."

Talking about the crash feels surreal for Tom. He feels on the verge of breaking into tears any moment, and he knows this is abnormal for him. He can't remember the last time he cried. And he knows he's never wept in front of Dale and Lily.

Tom wants to tell them about Pastor Marks, about the last-minute prayer. He wants to ask them about that—why their God would allow the man to die even though he called out to him and prayed and asked to be saved.

You prayed too.

But Tom prayed only for himself. The pastor prayed for all of them, including Tom.

It doesn't matter anyway. The prayers proved their

worth.

Another voice asks him a simple question he can't shake.

Then why are you still alive?

He wants to tell his aunt and uncle about these things, but he can't bring himself to do it. Habit prevails, and he remains in control of his emotions. Around ten he says he'd very much like to shower and then get some rest.

Lily finds him a fresh towel and washcloth and shows him to a room filled with pictures of Tom and his brother and items from their youth.

"What's this?" Tom asks. He doesn't remember this room from his previous visits.

"Just finished decorating it. We wanted to have a place for you and your brother if you ever came."

"What if we both came at the same time?" Tom asks with a smile, noting the one king-sized bed.

"That would be a miracle, just like you surviving that plane crash."

Lily leans up and kisses Tom on the cheek.

"I'm so sorry, Tom," she says.

"About what?"

"That you had to go through all that. And that you didn't feel comfortable enough to call your uncle and me."

"Lily," Tom says, calling her by her first name just like he always has, "I've already told you—I didn't want you guys worrying and calling up others and getting all upset. And I came to see you right afterward, right?"

She nods at him, her gaze unwavering. "You're sure you're okay?"

"No, I'm not okay. But I will be. I'll get through this."

"Maybe we should call your brother."

"Let's try tomorrow. I'd like to talk to him."

Lily smiles and lets her eyes fall to the carpeted floor.

"There are a lot of people I need to catch up with. Including you and Dale."

"We're always going to be here. You know that."

Tom nods and hugs his aunt good night.

Tom chuckles when he walks out of the bathroom adjoining the bedroom he'll be sleeping in and notices the clothes on his bed. It's a pair of sweatpants and a USC sweatshirt, probably the ones he sent his aunt and uncle during his college years. Or maybe ones he sent to Sean. He puts them on gratefully along with the thick flannel socks, keenly aware of the change of temperature at this higher altitude.

The room is a shrine to the Ledger boys. On the walls are framed portraits of Tom and Sean during all stages of their life. Sean, the natural athlete, is shown in a variety of action shots, from his days of playing quarterback during high school to his baseball years in college. Tom is represented by class photos and snapshots sent from the various places he had traveled.

Tom studies the pictures and notes the stark contrast between the carefree younger brother with a hint of naughtiness in the eyes and Tom's own serious, brooding persona. Even during his junior high and high school years, Tom always knew what he wanted. Not friends and popularity or fun and excitement. He wanted to make a life for himself, to make it on his own, and then to revel in well-earned luxuries.

Well, I've done a great job at that.

Homeless, jobless, with no friends to speak of and no love in his life—at least no one who knows it—this is what he has accomplished. After thirty-four years, this is what he has earned.

Thirty-four.

Am I really that old?

Tom tried to take it all in. The world's wonders. Its pleasures. Places. People. Dazzling treasures. The so-called finer things. He has all of these. Yet at thirty-four, he looks around and finds that he has nothing.

All he has is his life. A life that suddenly seems tentative and finite.

Tom knows he should be glad to be alive. Relieved. Thankful. But more than anything else, he is afraid.

The picture of that cocky, know-it-all kid on the wall, who looks fiercely into the camera and bears an uncanny resemblance to his face in the mirror, scares him. He never cared much about the people around him. He had goals and he was living for them. He was on his way toward never having to work another day in his life and having everything he would need to last him the rest of his life.

That life, he thinks in shame.

He thinks once more of his last-minute prayer. "Let me live." And he is here, living.

Tom is afraid and full of questions. Part of him still wants to ask Dale and Lily about them, but he doesn't want them to see his fear. He doesn't want them to preach at him or start trying to save him. He was already rescued from death once this week. Give him some time.

Tom keeps staring at all the mementos of two lives

lived. He knows he desperately needs to find Sean and tell him what happened. Sean is a younger, more immature version of himself—the id version of Tom, the person who does what he wants without looking ahead or thinking of the consequences. While Tom always did things with an end result in mind—for instance, the deal with Sloan was going to pay off for the rest of his life—Sean did foolish things without thinking, damaging himself and his body. Tom is afraid of what he'll find Sean up to.

In the corner of the room, Tom spots the computer monitor and keyboard. The CPU is under the desk. He suddenly has a thought, a strange compulsion, so he sits at the computer and turns it on to see if Dale and Lily have the Internet set up on it. Knowing them, the couple who've always had the latest electronic gadgets, Tom assumes there will be a connection. There is.

It's close to eleven at night, and Tom finds himself surfing the Internet, using the search engines to locate something specific. Or rather, someone.

He calls up his favorite search engine and types the name *Marks* in the blank line, then presses Enter. A listing of over ten thousand possibilities suddenly turns up on the screen. Tom narrows the search to *Pastor Kent Marks* and scrolls through the smaller list.

❖   ❖   ❖

Riverside Bible Church in Aurora, Illinois, appears to be an up-and-coming establishment, judging by its contemporary-looking and well-designed Web site. Tom locates it after scrolling through half a dozen other Web sites, mostly journal sites featuring articles by Kent Marks. The church Web site's menu links visitors to history pages, information about location and service times, a "For Kids" section, even a calendar for the upcoming week and a streaming video showing a regular service. Tom clicks on the heading he wants: Pastoral Staff.

Kent's photo is easy to find. He looks fresh out of college in the shot, wearing a blue blazer and striped tie. His light-brown hair is shorter and lighter in this photo and his face is tan, as if he'd come home from a beach vacation right before the photo was taken. Kent's grin is the same natural sort Tom noticed on the plane, the kind that allows you to talk freely to it, the kind that must make for a good pastor. Tom knows he's never worn a grin like this one. This kind of beam hides nothing. There is nothing hidden or hypocritical about it.

Tom clicks on Kent's photo, and the computer monitor fills with a bio page. Both intrigued and compunctious, Tom reads the blurb on Kent's life.

> Kent Marks loves teens. Some even call him a grown-up teen. That's why he is such a good fit in his pastoral role with HYACKS (High School Youth Advancing Christ's Kingdom through Students).
>
> Born and raised in Michigan, Kent came to the Chicagoland area to attend Wheaton College. He met and fell in love with his wife, Michelle, during those years at Wheaton. Kent and Michelle are the proud parents of Britta and Eli.
>
> Serving with Riverside Bible Church since 1999, the Marks have made an impression with high-school stu-

dents. Kent's philosophy is to "reach out, not preach out" to high schoolers. "High school is such an important time for kids," says Pastor Marks. "The world offers them so many different choices and temptations. My goal is to show that a life with Christ is one filled with joy and hope. I want to challenge high school students but also let them enjoy their age."

Every year, Pastor Marks leads a group of HYACKS on an overseas missions project. Last year, Marks brought forty-five high schoolers to the town of Jusibampo, Mexico, for outreach and building projects.

On his role as a pastor, Marks said that "serving the Lord can be fun, and my role with HYACKS proves that every day."

A life summed up by a few simple paragraphs, Tom thinks as he rereads the page. He carefully puts aside thoughts of how an article might sum up his life.

A captioned photo at the bottom of the article shows Kent with a group of students during one of their missions trips.

Such a different life, Tom reflects. Such a night and day comparison. A man working with a church, working with teenagers on top of that. Tom can't imagine spending time with older teens—know-it-all, MTV-watching, hormonally charged kids. He'd rather be put in prison or shot. And not only to work around them, but to preach to them?

Reach out, not preach out. The words form themselves in Tom's mind, but he has no idea where they came from. Probably something he heard as a kid.

He remembers the brief conversation he shared with

Kent and remembers that the man didn't preach to him at all. The prayer may have been a bit over the top, but considering the circumstances it was okay. At least Kent didn't hand him a pamphlet and then start talking about hell and eternal damnation.

That's what always gnawed at Tom whenever he heard one of these Bible-toting preachers on TV, waving their fingers and talking about hell and fire and brimstone (whatever brimstone was) and making everyone feel guilty. To Tom it always sounded phony, like a canned spiel. But Kent Marks seemed genuine. Even in the last minutes of his life, Kent acted out his faith in an admirable way. Tom knows he has to give this man credit. Kent didn't turn his back on the things he believed.

What did Tom do? He turned his back on his beliefs, or his lack of them, with a last-second prayer. Kent remained strong.

And he died being strong.

Tom reflects on the bio blurb again and thinks of a wife named Michelle and two kids named Britta and Eli. What happens to them now? Where does life take them? Presumably the people in the church will reach out and help them, but still. A husband and father is gone. Does it matter that they believe they'll see him again? Will that take away the pain?

And what about a boy who'll never even remember his father? What about this little girl who will grow up with one parent, hardly knowing the other, mixing her few memories with the bits and pieces that others tell her about his life?

Tom shuts off the computer and finds himself

immersed in emotion. He hates himself for being maudlin, for dwelling on Kent Marks, for feeling empty and remorseful.

Move on.

He refuses to let the plane crash alter his life. He won't allow it. He has spent too long building this life of his—

What life?

—and too much time preparing for this payoff. He needs to get his psyche back in order and stop wallowing in self-pity.

Move on, he tells himself again.

This visit with Dale and Lily—this resting stop of sorts—will be short. Maybe he'll call Sloan tomorrow and arrange another meeting time. Maybe he's just suffering from post-traumatic syndrome or whatever it's called. He needs to stop brooding about his past and about people like Allegra and Sean who are no longer in his life and never will be again.

I need to stop thinking about Kent Marks too, Tom tells himself.

But he can't help a simple thought—that Marks died and he didn't. The realization that this man who had so much was taken. And that Tom, who had messed up so many times, remained alive.

Another thought creeps into his mind. One he's tossed around for a while without actually facing it.

What if I died?

What would have happened? Nothing? Simply blackness, then nothing? This is what Tom believes, what he knows to be true, what he has spent years telling himself and others. But now, alone, away from his job and his familiar world, he wonders if he truly does believe it. A part of him whispers that there might be the possibility of something else. And what if, just what if, the man named Pastor Marks was right? What if his aunt and uncle were right? What if heaven awaited those with faith?

Then they must be right about the other thing too—that hell awaits those who have turned away from God. And did that apply to Tom? His lack of faith, the mistakes he's made throughout life, those ugly little secrets that books could be written about—what about all of that? He knows he's never been a drug user or a murderer, but what about a thief and a womanizer and a liar?

Stop this and go to bed.

Bed doesn't keep these thoughts away. Nor does sleep. He finds himself falling again, a knapsack on his back full of all the sins he's committed, the chute on his parachute broken, the air rushing by him as the ground grows bigger. And as hard as Tom tries to empty this sack on his back, he finds the mass inside growing, filling, overflowing. He is helpless to do anything except continue to fall to his death.

❖　　　　❖　　　　❖

Lily's voice asks Tom if he wants breakfast. Tom opens his eyes and is greeted by Lily's gentle smile.

"I'm starving," he says truthfully.

"Good then," Lily says in the dimness of the shaded room. "I'll make some waffles and bacon."

"Sounds great."

"How'd you sleep?"

"Like I was eighteen again."

"I can tell. It's almost ten."

Tom can't believe it. He's used to waking up at precisely six-thirty every morning. Even though he uses an alarm clock, he doesn't need to. His body flicks on the light switch at half past six and doesn't stop until late night. He can't remember the last time he slept through the morning.

Moments later, Tom sits at the round breakfast table with his aunt and uncle. They make small talk about the weather and Colorado Springs and the work Dale has done on the house. Tom shifts the conversation to Sean.

"So how's my little brother doing these days?"

Aunt Lily forces a grin, letting Dale answer.

"He's doing fine, I reckon. Did you hear he moved?"

"Moved? Where?" Tom asks.

"The friendly town of Las Vegas," Dale replies.

"What's he doing there?"

"Working in one of those big hotels. Where all the casinos are."

Tom laughs, thinking of his wilder younger brother in the wildest city in the United States.

"When's he going to get a real job?"

"He probably needs to finish school first," Dale says matter-of-factly as he finishes off his waffle.

"And you say you talked with him last week?"

"I think that's when it was," Lily replies. "He's as hard to get hold of as you."

Tom notes the look of sadness wrinkled over Lily's face.

"I know I should keep in touch with you guys more than I do," Tom says, knowing the apology sounds hollow, but meaning it all the same.

"We understand," Lily says unconvincingly.

"It's just—this last year. The last two actually. They've been bad."

"It's okay," his aunt replies. An awkward silence hangs in the air until she says, "So tell us more about why you decided to quit your job."

As if to save Tom from answering, the phone interrupts, and Aunt Lily moves from the table to retrieve it.

"Hello? Yes, who's calling? Well, okay."

Lily brings the cordless to Tom and shrugs her shoulders.

"Someone calling for you. Says his name is a Sloan."

Tom glares at the phone and takes it with hesitation.

"Do you know who that is?"

Tom nods and clears his throat. He puts a hand over the receiver and tells his aunt and uncle he'll take the call in the other room.

"Work stuff," he tells them. "Not sure how they got your number."

"Oh, it's fine," Dale replies, sipping on a cup of coffee.

Tom breathes in and out, in and out, as he walks to the dining room. He sits on one of the fancy chairs next to the dark-stained wood table and can feel his heart racing.

"This is Tom," he says into the mouthpiece.

"Mr. Ledger," the animated voice says, "it is a good thing to hear you're alive."

"What do you want?"

"I thought you might be a little more polite considering the circumstances."

"Why are you calling me here?"

"Why, Mr. Ledger, I think you know *why*. You have something that belongs to me."

"My aunt and uncle have nothing to do with this."

"And that is why I am talking to you, not to them," the man on the other end speaks.

Tom can picture the man he only knows as Mr. Sloan behind his mahogany desk, perhaps smoking a cigar, the dim light of one lamp illuminating the office.

"They don't know about any of it."

"As it should be," Sloan replies. "This is a private matter. Between you and me."

"I needed some time," Tom tells him.

"I can appreciate what you've gone through."

"I seriously doubt that."

"Mr. Ledger, I once had a charter plane go down due to weather. We landed in a field."

Tom grits his teeth and shakes his head. This man dares to compare that to what he and two hundred others went through?

"Did you almost die from breathing in fumes when you landed? Did you see any charred remains while you were down there?"

Silence, then the voice on the other end of the phone acquires a bit more of an edge.

"Because of this I'm granting you your wish of time. You've already been given more than enough."

"A day after I almost die and you send one of your men to pick me up?"

"It was a gesture, Mr. Ledger. I would think you might have appreciated it. I did not mean any harm. I had a hotel room ready for you with all the amenities. I simply wanted to guarantee you safe passage the rest of the way."

"Maybe you just wanted a guarantee."

"You're sounding very self-assured today. Might I remind you of the parameters of our deal?"

"Calling my aunt and uncle was not part of any deal."

"Neither was refusing to let me know where you were or what you were doing."

"I still have the information with me. Don't worry about it."

Another silence. "Were you still planning on giving it to me and explaining its contents to us?"

"Yes," Tom lies. "I just—I wasn't about to fly. I needed to get some family stuff back in order."

"We can make this simple, you know. All we need is

the date. And several hours of your time."

"I don't want any of this involving my aunt and uncle."

"That's why giving it to us as soon as possible would be beneficial."

Tom considers the possibilities and the choices. He still does not know what he's going to do regarding Sloan and the data he stole. The only thing he knows is that it can't involve Dale and Lily. They can't know anything about it.

"Give me two days."

"Mr. Ledger, my patience has already been well—"

"Two days. And I'll meet with your 'boys' in Vegas, okay? I'll give them everything you need, and then this will all be over. Saturday night. That's tomorrow night. I'll meet you guys there."

"Where?"

"I don't know. Call me on my cell."

"We have tried. Numerous times."

"I'll answer it this time," Tom replies. "Call me tomorrow after nine, and I'll tell you where."

"Might I remind you, Mr. Ledger, you're not the one calling the shots here?"

"And you're not the one holding priceless information."

"Again, you're not in any—"

"I know," Tom says. "Got it."

"Just keep that in mind. We'll be calling you tomorrow night. No more foolishness. We made a deal."

Tom clicks off the phone and heads back into the kitchen, where half his waffle remains uneaten.

"Everything okay?" Lily asks.

"Yeah. It was work. They had some questions about projects I was working on when I left."

"You look a bit pale," his aunt says, examining him all over. "Are you sure you're okay?"

"Maybe it's this high altitude," Tom made up. "I'm not used to the air around here."

"Your waffle's gotten cold. Can I fix you another one?"

Tom thinks about saying no, then decides why not. Suddenly his close monitoring of his caloric intake seems as meaningless as the deal he made with a man named Sloan weeks ago.

He remembers dark wood paneling. Everywhere. A mahogany desk. And a smile that could belong to a guardian angel if they existed.

Tom sat down on the leather couch that faced the desk. The man behind it, with thick eyebrows and a tanned face, played with a wireless mouse, two thin monitors in front of him probably displaying several pictures within pictures.

This is how the bad guy looks in a Bill Gates world, Tom remembers thinking.

Technology is everything, the man said once in an email. Technology is priceless. Yet, there is a price, and Sloan was going to pay him for it.

There was little small talk. Few pleasantries. For a few moments, Tom sat on the couch watching Sloan watch the monitors. A short man, lean and handsome, with exaggerated features. His dark gray hair was slicked back.

"Mr. Ledger. Please excuse me."

His congenial tone seemed to contradict his surroundings and his black dress shirt and khaki pants. He turned his head toward Tom and leaned back in his chair.

"Thanks for coming by."

He looked friendly, charming, a guy who liked to laugh.

A few seconds passed.

"So it's your turn now. Say something."

"I'm new at this," Tom replied.

"Fair enough. Jürgen says you have something I might be interested in."

"He is the one who contacted me."

"That's right. So talk specifics. When will it be released?"

"Not for another three or four years. At the earliest."

"And it's proven?"

"That's what the documents clarify. Test reports. Lab studies. All of that."

"How does a marketing director obtain this sort of information?" Sloan asked him.

"They just do."

"*They* can lie."

"People in labs talk. Files, information—it's not impossible to get if you know what you're looking for. Especially when it's not patented."

"So what are we talking about?" Sloan asked.

"Information. Documents. Hundreds of pages. Theories. Info that can help a man like you—info you can do something with."

"Do you know how revolutionary this can be? It's something phone companies, cable companies, the Internet—everyone will be using it."

"That's why I figured it's pretty valuable."

"And your price?"

"You name it," Tom told him.

A price was spoken as though it could be a listing of the weather. Tom nodded, knowing he'd only get one offer. But he accepted it. It was an offer for life—more money than he could ever earn in a lifetime. And tax free. All for simply getting a man he doesn't know some information on technology.

So much forgotten. So much he never knew.

In just a day's time, Tom realizes so much that he's neglected to remember about Dale and Lily. Their caring spirits that never seemed to resent having to raise two parentless kids. Their gentleness and willingness to go with the flow. Their love of other people.

Dale seems to have been born to serve others, and today he proves this to Tom by telling him of all the various projects he has going for neighbors and church people. Dale's retirement, Tom discovers, consists of volunteering at the thrift store two days a week, mowing the lawn at church, helping repair houses for the indigent, sometimes delivering Meals on Wheels "to those old folks." Lily helps with his projects, but she also makes sure they maintain an active social life. They go out with various church couples on a regular basis and host Sunday night coffee every evening after the service is over. They just got back from a trip to California to visit Dale's relatives.

What Tom realizes is that his aunt and uncle's life is full and rich, much more so than his own.

On this particular Friday, they take Tom to a mall so he can buy new clothes. Lily and Tom keep wrangling over who will pay for them. She wants to buy him things, and he keeps telling her no. Finally Tom gives in and lets her buy him a nice dark blue polo shirt. "An early Christmas present. Or a late one, since you weren't with us last Christmas."

Tom tries to remember where he was at Christmas, and all he can remember is clinking glasses with a woman named Naomi in the Walnut Room at the Chicago Marshall Field's.

After the mall, Lily and Dale show Tom their church and ask if he'll be staying with them through Sunday.

"Actually, I'm thinking about trying to hook up with Sean. I'm going to try to contact him today and maybe leave tomorrow."

A disappointed look crosses Lily's face, but Tom knows she won't protest. Being around Dale and Lily feels like old times, when he was much younger and wanted desperately to go out and conquer the world. They always treated him like an adult because he always acted like one. Dale and Lily rarely disciplined either Tom or Sean, and they gave them more freedom than most kids enjoyed. Looking back, Tom isn't sure this was the best way to go. Neither Tom nor Sean grew up to be shining role models. But Dale and Lily were never their parents, and they tried not to act like parents.

They arrive around five in the afternoon from the day in Colorado Springs. Lily gives Tom the number she has for Sean, and Tom sits down in the family room to call his long-lost brother. As he expects, Tom hears the sound of an answering machine.

"You probably wish I was here, but I'm not," his younger brother's voice says. "So since I'm not, leave a message if you want to. And maybe I'll call back. Or maybe not."

Tom shakes his head. Sean and his sense of humor. Everything in life is a joke to Sean. Even a simple recording machine.

"Sean. It's Tom. I'm at Dale and Lily's. Give me a call tonight, whenever you can. I'm thinking about driving to Vegas tomorrow and would love to hook up."

Tom is unsure whether Sean is even in town. But if he gets the message, he'll probably call Tom back. Regardless of how out of control he's been in his life, Sean always looked up to Tom and liked being around him. Tom wishes he can say the same about himself. But the truth is that Tom tended to keep his family contacts to a minimum. He always wanted to go out and find success in the world and then come back and show off his achievements to his family and find them proud of him. Somewhere along the way, Tom knows that he forgot to come back.

Around five-thirty that evening the national news comes on, and Tom finds himself hearing more details of National Flight 2171. For a few minutes he watches footage of the plane tumbling across a runway strip before ripping apart and bursting into flames. He sees weeping burn victims, stretchers with bodies being pulled out of cornfields, family members embracing with tears. Details about the loss of hydraulics and the heroics of the pilot and the copilots as they worked feverishly to land the plane anyway make Tom sick. He grabs the remote and turns off the television. The silence soothes him a bit, but the memories and the images in his head remain.

"You okay?"

Tom jerks and turns around to see Dale.

119

"Yeah."

"Gotta be something, going through that."

"I still can't bring myself to watch the news. Part of me tries to just turn it off, turn off everything. I can't erase the memory."

"It's going to be a long time before you get over it. If ever."

Tom nods.

"Can I ask you a question, Tom? A personal one?"

"Sure."

"When was the last time you called Allegra?"

Tom smiles and looks down to the white, spotless carpet of the family room.

"A while."

"What's a while?" Dale asks.

"Quite a while. Years."

"I was just wondering—wanted to know if you called her after this."

"No."

Dale nods and waits for Tom to say something, but then apparently decides to leave it at that. He tells Tom he's going to get the mail.

Tom thinks about Allegra again. Since he left her, how many women have been in his life? A dozen, maybe more. All meaningless relationships that consisted of mutual attraction with no strings attached. Some of these became a little more involved, usually when there was sex involved. But none of them mattered.

He doesn't feel guilt or shame for feeling this way. It's just the truth. None of them ever mattered nor could they ever give him what he was looking for. Another Allegra. She could not be duplicated.

She still can't be.

Tom wonders if it is time to contact her. He doesn't know how long it has been, but he knows it's been too long. Too long without a word. Without a single word.

So much forgotten. But it's begun to start coming back to him.

Her dark-green oval eyes and the full, rounded lips and the way she gleamed anytime she spotted him. Years of being together, and she still always shot him that magnificent gaze that said she belonged to him and he belonged to her.

For so long it seemed almost perfect. But Tom felt something was missing. He believed he could find the missing part if he looked hard enough and tried hard enough—no matter how far away the search took him.

Years later, Tom knows there is no missing part—or at least no missing part he can go out and find. The missing part was an insecurity deep inside of Tom, a part of him he didn't know could never be fulfilled, no matter how much life gave him. It didn't exist in a person or a place or any possessions he could own.

Tom believes now that this insecurity will be there for life. He has no need to keep looking, but he's learned that too late. He will probably never see or talk to Allegra again. And even if he does, he knows she will never take him back.

"Zoning out on us?" Lily asks him as she comes into the brightly lit family room. Late-day sunlight pours in through the tall windows on the west wall, and she holds up a hand to shelter her eyes.

"Yeah, a little," Tom replies.

"I was thinking. Do you want to go out to eat at Michelangelo's?"

"That's still around?"

Lily nods. "And still as wonderful as ever."

"It's been a long time since I've been there."

"Remember the first time we took you?"

Tom smiles. "How can I forget? I'd love to go."

❖   ❖   ❖

I want you guys to meet Allegra," Tom said as he steered her toward their table.

The look on Dale's and Lily's faces amused Tom. He could see they were both surprised and overwhelmed by Allegra—partly because they hadn't known she was African-American, but more because of her astonishing, dominating beauty, a kind that turned many men's heads as she strolled by them. She wore heels and a long black skirt, with a tight white top that revealed flawless bare shoulders and slender arms. Braids of ebony hair poured down across her shoulders to her back.

Dale and Lily stood as Tom and Allegra neared the table. Dale took her hand as Lily smiled.

"I hope your trip went well," Lily said.

"Very well," Allegra's silken voice replied. "I don't usually like to fly, but Tom talked my ear off."

"That's because you kept asking me questions."

"About what?" Dale asked.

"About you guys," Tom replied with a wide grin. "She's been nervous."

Allegra's green eyes widened to tell Tom to be quiet.

"I told you they're harmless," Tom said.

"We've heard quite a bit about you, Allegra," Lily said, sitting next to her.

"Uh-oh."

"Tom rarely tells us things, so when he told us all about you, we knew you had made quite an impression on him."

"We weren't even sure we'd see him this Christmas," Dale said, "much less bring you."

"I told him we should visit you guys," Allegra replied with a reflective, soft tone. "He works too hard as it is."

"So you got off a whole week?"

Tom nodded his head at his aunt. "If I didn't, I'd lose it in the new year."

"How is BSI?"

"Fine, I guess."

Tom said little more about the job he loathed, a sales position where every few months the powers that be would decide which salesmen they'd keep on. Selling software, including computers and technology, for Bennett Systems Incorporated brought Tom about as much excitement and satisfaction as working for a used-car business. He had been at BSI even before earning his MBA. A year later, at twenty-five years old, Tom felt he needed and deserved more.

"So, Allegra," Lily's cheerful voice began, "tell us how exactly you met Tom."

"I've already told them."

"But you just said you met her in a restaurant while she was waiting on your table."

"He's quite the romantic, huh?" Allegra said, nudging Tom.

"There has to be more," Lily said.

"Tom, in fact, is *quite* romantic. It's just a secret no one can know."

"Please." Tom rolled his eyes and laughed.

"I used to work at a restaurant called The Wharf. There was a group of about six men who came in for a business dinner and all ordered steak and lobster—the works. They were quite rowdy and a bit rude, too."

"Typical," Tom said.

"Including Tom?" Aunt Lily asked.

"No, not Tom."

"She doesn't really even remember me."

"I do too."

"She just remembers me as the young kid at the table."

"Well, he was around these forty- and fifty-year-old guys drinking scotch and whiskey. He didn't have anything to drink. I remember that. Mr. In Control, just like always. Near the end of the meal, one of the men said something to me, and Tom came up afterward to apologize."

"My boss hit on her," Tom clarified. "They'd all been hitting on her all night long, but my boss went a bit too far."

Tom looked at Allegra and shook his head. "Thank God I don't answer to Rick anymore."

"I was used to those sorts of things."

"Rick was pretty nasty. Allegra, of course, still smiled and flirted with them—"

"I didn't flirt with them," she insisted.

"Well, she got a nice tip anyway."

"I did."

"So after dinner I lingered around—"

"Hey," Aunt Lily said. "Isn't Allegra telling this story?"

"Oh yeah. Sorry. You keep telling it."

"The men stayed around for a while and ended up being my last table. After they left, I was checking out—ringing up my charges and counting my cash—when Tom came back in, looking so cute and friendly."

"Nice," Tom said.

"I've always thought he kinda resembled a young Tom Cruise, don't you think?" Allegra asked.

"I'm quite a bit taller than him," Tom replied, having heard that one before. "It's only because of the name."

Allegra pretended to whisper across the table to Lily and Dale. "I thought he was adorable, to be honest." She smiled and continued in her regular voice. "He apologized for the men, especially his boss, and I told him it was nothing, that I got that sort of thing all the time. Then Tom said something I'll always remember."

"What?" Lily asked.

"He looked at me earnestly with those stern eyes of his and said, 'Well, you shouldn't. Just because you're stunning doesn't mean guys should treat you that way.' He said this not in a way that was meant to pick me up or flatter me—"

"It just came out," Tom said.

"Anyway, he checked to be sure I got a decent tip, and I thanked him and was still unsure what to say about his compliment. It meant a lot to me. Then he left, and that could have been the end of it all."

"So what happened?" Lily asked again, this story brand-new to her.

Allegra nodded to Tom, who began to speak.

"I remember getting in my car and starting it up, then thinking about Allegra. I hadn't dated anyone for a while, mostly because of work. I remember thinking, *When's the next time I'm going to run into someone like her?* So I shut off the car and went back into the restaurant."

"It was so sweet," Allegra said.

"I went up to her and said—"

"I can say what you said."

"Okay."

Allegra's smile filled her face, her dimple showing just below two lone freckles on her cheek.

"He came up to me and apologized for bothering me. Then he said that it was probably not his place to ask something, especially since he didn't know me. He gave me some nice compliments and then asked if I wouldn't mind having someone else wait on us for a meal, maybe lunch or dinner."

"I said a little more than that," Tom said.

"I said you paid me some nice compliments."

"I went back into the restaurant and told her she was probably one of the most beautiful women I'd ever seen in my entire life. I said something like, 'Look, I know that's a line, and I also know that's pretty trite and superficial. All I ask is for a chance—a chance for you to sit down with me for a meal or a dessert and just get to know me and see if you like what you see.' And she gave me a shrug and said why not."

"I thought to myself, I already liked what I saw."

"I gave her my number, and sure enough, she called a few days later."

"And I haven't been able to get rid of him yet," Allegra joked.

"That was about two years ago. A lot has changed since then."

She turned to his aunt and uncle with a playful glance and pretended to whisper. "I keep telling him he's in love with me. He just won't admit it yet."

❖   ❖   ❖

Nine years after the dinner where he introduced Allegra to Dale and Lily, Tom sits in the same restaurant and remembers how long it has been. He left Allegra three years later, when he was twenty-eight years old. When he thought he knew what sort of decision he was making, breaking off "baggage" and leaving everything that meant something to him behind for something more tangible.

One couldn't see and stockpile love and family, Tom used to think. Commas on a bank statement—now there was something you could hold on to. Portfolios and savings accounts and investments in art and real estate. At BSI, Tom had been going nowhere fast. And somehow, in some sickening and ill-hearted way, Tom came to equate his life in California at BSI with his relationship with Allegra.

She told me she would never move away from her family, Tom remembers.

And just as easily as words are spoken, Tom left her.

Tom looks across the table past the gentle, warm candlelight to his aunt.

"Have you guys heard from Allegra any?"

They've been at the restaurant almost an hour, and talk has breezed by on many subjects, but Allegra hasn't been one of them. They've been safe subjects, ones Dale and Lily know are not off-limits.

"It's been a while. Perhaps a few months."

A nail rips into Tom's gut. "Are you serious?"

"She sends us cards every now and then. Every Christmas. And sometimes she writes to us, either by letter or email. Nothing much. Just keeping in touch."

"Do you talk about me?"

Lily shakes her head. "We don't talk. Just write. And only every now and then. And no—I mean, I rarely talk about you. What would I say? I hardly talk to or hear from you as it is."

"Where is she? And how—"

"She's still in California. She lives close to Newport Beach."

Tom gazes across the restaurant, thinking but not knowing exactly what he's thinking about, simply trying to get a grasp on the fact that Allegra is still alive—

And why shouldn't she be?

—and that she's kept in touch with his aunt. That she's in California—

But you knew she'd probably always be there.

—and that's she's doing well.

"Is she doing well?" Tom asks.

"I think so."

"And she doesn't—does she ever ask anything about me?"

"No. Not in that way. Tom, it's been six years I think since you went to Chicago. You never mention her. I just—she was such a dear young woman." Lily eyes Dale with a suspicious glance. "I just assumed—I know you don't like talking about her."

Tom nods. "I know."

"Every time I've brought her up in the past—"

"I know, okay?" Tom's voice is sharper than he intended.

Dale and Lily both look shyly away from Tom as he gains a grip on his emotions.

"Look, I'm sorry," Tom says. "It's just—I guess I just assumed you hadn't heard from her."

"I wasn't trying to deceive you, Tom."

"No, I know. I really haven't thought of Allegra for a long time. I think I consciously didn't. I just wanted to move on with my life. It was just—when I was on the plane and it was going down—you take a look at things in your life. I thought of a lot of stuff I hadn't thought of for a long time."

"I thank God that you made it out of that crash," Lily says.

"It's like I thought of all these things I should've done. I was hoping for another chance. But . . . do you guys believe that a man can really have a second chance after living half a life doing what he's wanted to do?"

They gaze at him for a long moment before answering.

"Of course," his aunt says in a voice just above a whisper.

"We're all given many chances in life," his subdued uncle says.

"But I'm talking a second chance. A legitimate second chance. I mean—I'm thirty-four years old. And things—like Allegra. Can someone start over again with that sort of thing behind them?"

"I believe you can. But that doesn't mean you can undo the past."

Tom nods. "When I walked away from that plane—when I woke up the next morning and saw the sunrise and breathed in air, it was like nothing I'd ever done before. I just feel like I've been overly melodramatic about everything since then."

"Life is a gift we're given," Dale says.

Tom laughs at his reflective and introspective uncle. *Some things never change,* he thinks.

"You know, King David in the Bible was given a second chance."

"That's a little different from what I'm talking about," Tom replies.

"Is it?"

"Well, a Bible story—that's not the kind of thing I'm talking about."

"David committed adultery with another man's wife and killed that man to cover up his sin."

"This is David—the same guy who killed the giant? What's his name—Goliath?"

"The same. But this was years later."

Tom shakes his head.

"David asked for God's forgiveness after everything he did. You should read Psalm 32."

"That's the Bible, right?" Tom asks.

Dale nods. "It's a song where David is baring his soul and talking about being given another chance in life. And he was given one."

"Yeah, but like I said, it's not like I suddenly had this yearning to become a missionary or anything like that."

"You're talking about a second chance. Another chance

at life, to make up for mistakes you made. Right?"

Tom nods at his uncle, unsure that what he's saying really applies and not even sure what all his mistakes have been. The only one he knows for certain, beyond any doubt, is the mistake he made with Allegra years ago.

"It's probably too late," Tom says.

"Forgiveness is only a millisecond away."

Headlights pierce the darkness of the Colorado countryside near Dale and Lily's home. The Jeep Cherokee moves steadily, rarely passing any sign of life or light. Dale is driving, with Tom in the front passenger seat. Aunt Lily sits behind the two of them. For a while they ride in silence.

"That religious stuff you always talk about," Tom begins, pausing for a second before continuing on, "do you ever have doubts?"

"I don't know," Dale says. "Not that I know of."

"I do," Aunt Lily says from the back. "The same way I get angry when I know I shouldn't. It's like that. It's something that I get but I know better."

"But you guys know deep down that it's the truth, right?"

"Yes," Dale says without hesitation.

Lily hesitates, then says, "That's what faith is all about."

Tom remembers another conversation he had recently about faith.

The Jeep slows at a pulsing yellow light that throbs like a heartbeat. A gas station on the corner brightens the dark of night they drive through.

"How can it be so easy for you?" Tom's voice asks, his eyes staying straight ahead on the road.

"It's a matter of being filled with the Spirit," his uncle replies. "Reading the Word."

"That means nothing to me."

"Tom—"

"I'm just being honest," Tom replies to his aunt. "The 'Spirit'—the 'Word'—I just don't get any of that."

"They are real things."

"Not to me."

"Look around you," Dale tells him. "Everywhere. There are signs of God everywhere."

"How come all I see is darkness?" Tom asks.

Silence fills the car, then Uncle Dale clears his throat. No one says a word.

"You know I prayed right before the plane went down. I was afraid. Others prayed too. So why would God answer *my* prayer and not theirs?"

Tom feels a hand on his shoulder from his aunt. Neither says a word still.

"I thought that something divine might happen. That I might die and realize that God was real. Instead I woke up and ran out of the plane and saw death all around me."

"But you were saved," Dale says.

"I saved myself. I was the one who got myself out of the plane. Jesus didn't pick me up with his hand and put me safely down on the ground."

"Why is it so hard to think God might have saved your life that day?"

"There's no reason why he'd save someone like me," Tom says.

"I can say the same thing," Dale says.

"But you weren't in a plane accident."

"But I'm a sinner, Tom. I've done things I'm not proud of. And God forgave me. He saved me from myself."

"Come on—you're one of the good guys. You haven't done anything to need saving for."

"We all have. The apostle Paul used to kill Christians before God saved him."

"Come on," Tom says loudly in frustration. "I don't want to hear about Davids and Pauls and all that stuff. I'm talking now. The year 2002. Today."

"What I'm trying to say is, God can still save any sinner."

"You just love preaching it up, don't you?" Tom asks his uncle. Part of him knows the accusation is unfair, but he says it anyway.

"I'm not trying to preach, Tom. I'm just telling you what is on my heart."

"Really."

"Yes."

"Well, tell me this one thing. If this is what's *on your heart,* why didn't you ever talk about this with Sean and me?"

The question lingers, with Aunt Lily's hand still on his shoulder, and is left more or less unanswered. Dale says something about the two boys never listening, and Lily says something about letting them make their own decisions. It doesn't matter to Tom—not anymore. He is too old to change his beliefs now, and the second chance he's talking about has nothing to do with God and Paul and David or the Bible.

They ride down a dirt road, gravel spitting up behind

them. The subject is done, and Tom feels no closer to having any other faith besides his belief in himself.

❖　　　　❖　　　　❖

The refrigerator door invites a warm glow into the kitchen. Tom finds a container of rainbow sherbet as expected and leaves the freezer open, taking a few bites with a small spoon. Satisfied at this midnight sampling, Tom returns the room to darkness and slips outside onto the deck. The chalk-white thumbprint of the moon reveals itself amidst a dotted sky. He sits in a plastic chair with a foam-padded seat cushion and leans back to gape at the stars.

He remembers feelings of isolation living here with Dale and Lily growing up. They lived closer to the Springs back then, closer to civilization and neighboring families, but he still always felt like an outsider, detached from the rest of the world. Everything that was happening on the news and written about in newspapers and magazines seemed to be happening away from their calm, routine lives. Tom always felt lonely when he looked up into the faraway audience of stars.

Tonight he feels different. He finds himself wishing he could go back, wishing he could experience a life without any baggage. He wishes he didn't know all the things he knows about the world beyond this deck and its endless stars. He wishes someone stood behind them. Someone in charge of it all.

"You hear me up there?" he asks in a hushed, mumbled tone.

If only it could be so easy.

He opens the cell phone, and its orange screen greets him. He presses a button to retrieve the menu for messages, then he listens to the voice mails he knows will be there.

He deletes several messages from Sloan, then hears a familiar voice screaming at him as music competes in the background.

"Speak of the devil," his younger brother says. "So you're gonna come out and lose some money? I'll be around, so give me a call as soon as you get in. How long has it been?"

His younger brother laughs as the message ends. Same Sean. Could have been five or even ten years ago. Some things will never change. Some people won't either.

What about you?

He listens to the final message on his voice mail.

"Tom. I hope you get this voice mail. Listen to me—you have to call me as soon as you get this. It doesn't matter what time. Just call. We have to talk."

Jürgen's normally subdued tone is gone. In its place echoes the sounds of alarm, maybe something else. Tom knew he would be hearing from Jürgen. He's curious what he'll say.

He scrolls through the addresses and finds the name. He knows him only as Jürgen. He doesn't know if that's a first or a last name or even if it's real. He's only met him face-to-face once, and that was during his visit with Sloan.

The number is another cell phone. Jürgen probably has it in hand since it only rings twice before being answered with a "Where are you?"

"Colorado Springs."

"I heard about the plane crash," Jürgen says. "You weren't hurt?"

"Barely touched."

"That's unbelievable."

"Part of me still doesn't believe I walked away."

"Sloan said he spoke with you today."

Four sentences before getting down to business. Just like that.

"And I told him I'd make the delivery in Vegas."

"It's not supposed to go down like this."

"The crash wasn't supposed to happen either. Think about that?"

"Of course. Look, I'm sorry. I'm just telling you this for your own good. I don't think you understand everything that's going on."

"You told me I didn't need to."

"And you don't," an animated Jürgen replies.

"I see I didn't wake you up tonight."

"There's a lot riding for me on this too, you know."

"I didn't tell anyone I changed my mind."

Jürgen curses and says it's a good thing.

"I know I should've delivered everything by now, but it wasn't my fault."

"So then what was with the whole escape-from-Alcatraz deal?"

Tom laughs. "What's that supposed to mean? Who told you that?"

"You slipped away."

"I almost died. Don't you get that?"

"There are people that don't care about that. Don't you get that?"

"I do."

"I think you need to understand it better."

"What was that?" Tom asks.

"What?"

"Is that a threat?"

"Of course not." A sigh in the phone. "I'm not the one in charge here. *I* don't make threats. Look, this was supposed to be simple. I get you involved, you do the deed, deliver the package, we all come out on top."

"That easy, right?" Tom feels his forehead dot with sweat from the tension racing inside of him.

"People understand about everything."

"I don't think they do."

"Well I do, Tom. I'm trying to. But you've got to understand—you're dealing with something massive. You're dealing with something that involves billions of dollars. You're dealing with the future, Tom. This isn't some little thing we've got here."

"Where are you now?"

"What does that matter?"

"I'm just wondering."

"Where do you think?" Jürgen asks.

"Somewhere in Nevada?"

"Yep. I'm going to be seeing you sometime soon."

"So I just give it to you, and the rest is taken care of?"

"It's that easy. It *can* be that easy."

"Yeah, I guess so," Tom replies.

A silence fills the line.

"Tom?"

"Yeah?"

"What's going on?"

Tom gazes up again at the cold, stony glow of the moon.

"Most people don't just survive something like a plane crash and go on with life as normal."

"There's nothing normal about this. You were already involved in a crash before you even set foot on that plane."

"I love the way your tone changes."

Jürgen reels off a few profanities at Tom. "Wake up, man. What do I have to tell you to get this through to you? It's not about me or you. I'm not the one with the issues."

"Things will happen as planned."

"They'd better," Jürgen says. "For your sake."

The line clicks off, and Tom stares back out across the treetops to the infinite, inscrutable sky.

How could he have ever guessed that the big world outside Colorado Springs would lead him into this mess? How could he have imagined the bigger world was somehow better?

I'm going to make it better, Tom vows. *I got off that plane for a reason. I know that for sure.*

There is a reason. There has to be a reason. He believes with all his heart there must be a reason.

He just doesn't know what that reason is.

❖   ❖   ❖

Here's a little something for the drive." Lily hands him a small cooler.

"No, really, I can't take this," Tom replies.

Lily nods firmly. "It's a pretty long drive. You'll get thirsty."

"That's why they have McDonald's." But Tom realizes it's a lost cause, and he takes the small cooler with a smile of thanks.

The blue sky is scattered with cotton puffs as the three of them stand in the warm sun on the driveway. The Ford's top is down, with a suitcase Lily and Dale gave Tom in the trunk. Tom looks at his aunt and uncle as they stand together on the driveway, watching him put the cooler on the floor of the front passenger seat.

"Thank you, guys," Tom says, as he gives both of them hugs.

Lily smiles and wipes away tears from her eyes as she hugs him longer than expected.

"Take care of yourself," she says.

Tom wonders why Lily is so upset, but he doesn't want to mention anything to make matters worse.

"Let us know when you get situated in California,"

Dale says.

Tom nods.

"Tell your brother to call us, too," Lily urges. "Tell him to come see us."

"I will. Who knows what he's up to?"

"And thank you."

Tom looks at his aunt and gives her a puzzled face.

"What for?"

"For coming by here. For feeling like you still could."

"I know it's been a while. But I promise it won't be that long again."

"You sure?" Lily asks.

"You'll see me again. Very soon. I promise."

Tom slides into the convertible and nods at them before taking off.

"Be careful," his aunt says, a comment as routine as waking up and finding her in her robe in the kitchen.

❖   ❖   ❖

Four hours into the drive on the hot Saturday, Tom opens the cooler and finds a lemonade Snapple drink. He downs a third of it as he drives at a steady pace down the highway. He starts to close the lid on the cooler, but a plastic bag catches his attention. He picks it out of the drinks and ice and sees an envelope tucked inside of it.

With his thighs guiding the steering wheel, his hands open up the wrapped and taped plastic. He slips a card out of the envelope with his name on it. As he opens the card, something flies out of it and lands on the back floorboard of the car. Tom slows the car down and tries to read the card.

The outside is floral and has the words *Thank You* on it. Inside is a note in Aunt Lily's careful hand.

Dear Tom,

It's been a delight to see you again and have you spend time with us. We cannot say how thankful we are that you walked away from the accident. There is no way we can know how you feel about it, but we want you to know that we're here if you want to talk about anything.

Thank you for your candor during our discussion about God the other night. Please don't completely give up on believing in him. I know this is something you don't accept. But Tom, I believe God let you survive the plane crash for a reason.

Enclosed is a photo I was hesitant to give you while you were here. It was a photo I received from Allegra last Christmas. Maybe I shouldn't give it to you. Allegra's life has changed in many ways. I know she was a part of your past, and that it is none of our business. I just thought you might like to have the photo.

Please know you will continue to be in our thoughts and prayers. We love you, Tom. We hope you know that. We wish the best for you in everything you do.

Lily and Dale

The Mustang slows down and Tom directs it onto the shoulder of the highway. He reaches back and finds the photo still resting on the floor of the backseat. *It almost slipped away,* he thinks as he grabs the three-by-five snapshot and studies it.

It's unmistakably Allegra, with her golden features and shining, mysterious eyes. Her hair is shorter and straight, cut just above her shoulders. The picture shows her by a Christmas tree, alone, smiling as she used to when she nudged him awake in the mornings. She almost looks untouchable, like some famous movie star on the pages of *People* magazine. Yet Tom knows Allegra's beauty exists not in her remarkable features but in the fact that she never believed there was anything remarkable about them.

That's why she ended up with me, Tom thinks.

And she should have been the one to leave me, not vice versa.

He can't take his eyes off the picture of Allegra in the red and green sweater, looking composed and natural in front of the camera. He reads through Aunt Lily's note again, too, wondering what she meant by saying "Allegra's life has changed in many ways." Is it Tom's place to know how it's changed? Is it his place even to look at this photo again?

A thought pricks at his conscience, a tiny voice that he began hearing the last few days.

No, he tells himself. *I can't go see her again. I wouldn't even know how to find her.*

Tom sticks the photo and the card back in the envelope. A gust of emotion blasts him like a semi blowing past at one hundred miles an hour.

Stop it, Tom. Get a grip. Come on.

He clasps the steering wheel as tightly as he can and doesn't believe what is happening. He cannot even recognize it. Before shifting the gear back into drive, a finger reaches up to his eyes and wipes them quickly. He dries it on his shirt.

Not now. Not after all this time.

The Mustang finds its way back onto the highway. Tom quickly brings it up to a coasting speed of ninety miles per hour. He looks down at the envelope and puts it in the glove compartment to make sure it doesn't blow away.

He drives west and wonders if this road will lead to Allegra.

❖   ❖   ❖

A million sparkles of light spread out in front of him, like a fully decorated Christmas tree set on fire. The highway behind him is a dark inkblot, the stretch of desert around him murky vastness. The sun disappeared an hour ago, and in its place is a glittering city known as Las Vegas. Its pearly gates await his arrival.

Tom glances at the clock and reads 8:57. He knows his phone is on, resting on the seat next to him. The only sound bearing down on him is the swirling of wind and the hum of his car's engine. He expects the call from Sloan's men any minute, yet still is unsure whether he'll take it.

All day, while driving, Tom has considered his options. He's even questioned whether he has options, but a feisty voice inside of him tells him that he *always* has options, that he can do whatever he wants. And right now, he doesn't want to have anything to do with Sloan anymore.

It's not a matter of ethics and conscience. That's what he tells himself. It's not because he feels guilt. It's something else.

Something changed after that plane went down.

Tom doesn't know exactly what changed or how it happened. He does know that, before, he carried a map for his life in his head, and all he had to do was look at it to see where he should go next. Most recently the map said he should go west. Head west and find the promised land. Find wealth and happiness. Head west and do a simple deed and spend the rest of his life on nothing but pleasure.

But somehow, on his way west, the plane took a detour and made a crash landing. Somehow, for some reason, Tom escaped with his life. And a damaged road map he's having trouble reading.

This isn't about the plane or a road map, Tom thinks as the wind whips his hair and as the city limits of Vegas come closer in view.

The phone rings. Once.

Tom picks up the phone and holds it in his hand.

Head west, and you'll have everything you have ever wanted.

Another ring.

Pick it up and follow their instructions and be done with it.

Another ring.

Just answer it and see what they have to say.

Another.

Tom stares at the cell phone as the ringing stops and his voice mail kicks in.

He keeps driving. The phone rings again.

He stares straight ahead. He doesn't know why, but he's aware he's made his decision. A man named Sloan isn't controlling his life. A man named Sloan and his partners aren't calling the shots. Tom can back out of this if he wants to, and he wants to. This isn't the Mafia he's talking about, not some drug lord or terrorist. This is a businessman interested in money. That's the only issue in any of this—money. And suddenly, for the first time in Tom's life, money doesn't seem to matter.

The photo in the glove compartment, Tom thinks. *That's what matters.*

A woman somewhere on the West Coast. A woman he left years ago and never talked to again. A woman he once promised to love the rest of his life.

The phone rings stop again. They start again.

Would you ever take me back? Tom wonders. *Do you still have feelings for me?*

Tom lets the phone keep ringing and knows there's no turning back. He isn't doing this for Allegra, or for Dale and Lily, or for anyone else. It's for him. It's his decision.

There has to be a reason why, Tom muses. A reason why he survived the plane crash. A reason why he was given another chance.

If I've been given a second chance, what is it for?

A second chance to love? A second chance for a future, for a family? A second chance at a life he turned away from?

Tom turns off his phone as the ringing begins again. He doesn't know what the second chance is for. But one thing is for certain. He was given the choice of whether or not to go through with this corporate thievery, and he knows now he isn't going to do it. Regardless of the consequences.

❖   ❖   ❖

Sean Ledger walks into the diner and scans the room with expressionless disregard. He wears jeans and an untucked white button-down shirt, with his bare chest showing through three open buttons. His dark hair is curlier than Tom's and unkempt as always. Tom is startled by how skinny he appears. Sean sees him and shakes his head as he collapses in a booth across from him.

"What's with this?"

"What do you mean?" Tom wonders about the attitude.

"You want to meet me *here?* What is this place anyway?"

"You've never been to the Hearts Diner?" Tom asks with a grin.

"No. And I don't plan to come back either."

"Come on. Relax."

"You're the one who should relax. Come on, man. I thought we could go out tonight. Have some fun."

Tom studies his brother for a moment. "We can. And will. I just couldn't come over to your place."

"Why?"

"Later. I'll tell you in a little while."

"Okay."

A waitress comes. Sean simply shakes his head and holds out a hand in a "Whoa, there" gesture. Tom gives her a few dollars to cover his soda.

"So what's going on?" Tom asks.

"Nothing."

"You're living in Vegas, Sean. I'm sure something's going on."

"Well, yeah. Something's always going on. But . . . you know."

"Where are you working?"

"The Mirage." Sean fidgets with his hands, apparently uncomfortable at sitting in one place.

"Doing what?"

"Help run some of the shows. Mind if I smoke?"

"I don't, but they might."

"Oh yeah. Are you wanting to stay here?"

Tom shakes his head and follows his younger brother out of the diner that's part of a hotel off the main strip of Las Vegas. He decided it would be safer to call and meet Sean here instead of risking being followed to Sean's apartment.

"I took a cab here," Sean says when they emerge into the orange-lit night. He lights up a cigarette as they walk down the street.

"What kind of shows do you help run? Ones with girls?"

Sean laughs, a familiar cackle that always sounds like he's told a dirty joke. It's the same deep chuckle Sean used to offer whenever he got in trouble and Dale and Lily tried talking with him.

"They're shows during the day. For tourists like you."

"You dress up like a pirate or something?"

"Yeah. That's me."

"What do you do?"

"Sound for the shows. That sort of thing."

They pass a casino with its open entryway and its luring lights and music and crowds.

"What?"

"I didn't say anything," Tom says.

"That nod you gave me."

"I didn't say anything."

"You gonna give me a lecture about college and all that?"

"It's been a while since I did."

"People don't change," Sean replies.

"So—whatever happened to ASU?"

"It's still there. Doing fine."

"Too much for you?"

"Too boring. Guess I'm just not the scholarly type."

Tom wants to tell his brother about the plane crash, about everything that's happened since. But something inside of him tells him to hold off.

"You always liked to come here," Tom says, changing the subject. "I wasn't surprised to hear you'd moved."

"I live in the hotel."

"You sleep much?"

"Enough."

"You don't look so healthy."

Sean finishes his cigarette and flings it into the street. "That's Lily talking."

"When'd you last see them?"

"They didn't tell you? I don't know. More recent than you had before your little trip."

"They send their love and all of that."

Sean stops and turns to Tom. "What are you doing here?"

"Visiting you."

"Yeah, but why? Is there something going on?"

"I was on a business trip of sorts and stopped by Dale and Lily's."

"It's not like Vegas is next door."

"It's close enough. I'm driving to California anyway."

Sean's dark brown eyes scrutinize Tom. He lights another cigarette. "Are you in trouble?" he asks.

Tom wipes his forehead. Even near midnight, the desert heat is getting to him.

"A bit, yeah."

"Anything I should know?"

They pass another large casino, this one only a block away from the downtown strip. Tom points inside.

"Ever been in this one?"

"They're all the same. They take your money."

"Want to get something to eat?"

"It's eleven-twenty," Sean replies.

"You've had your share to drink tonight, haven't you?"

"What's that mean?"

"I can smell your breath from here."

"Ah, the older and wiser big brother returns."

"Yeah, to the younger ignoramus," Tom says.

"Hey, you're the one in trouble. Yeah, let's go inside. It looks harmless enough."

❖   ❖   ❖

A cloud of Marlboro Light stings Tom's eyes. A steady beat of classic 70s rock plays in the background as Tom and Sean sit at a round table. Tom neglects his beer while his younger brother works on another rum and coke.

Tom finishes up telling his brother what he's done and wonders if Sean will remember any of this tomorrow. His sibling's eyes are glassy and red. Every now and then they seem weighted down, and they shut for longer than the millisecond of a blink. Sean stares and even nods, but Tom suspects he's simply nodding off.

"Want to go back to your place?" he prompts.

"The big brother, in trouble," Sean says with a wiry chuckle.

"It's not really trouble, like I said. There are just some issues."

"So go through it. What's the big deal?"

"You're a big help," Tom replies.

"You can give me some while you're at it."

"When was the last time you got some rest?"

"You don't sleep around here. Not at night, anyway. You know, I wake up sometimes at eight or nine—"

"In the morning?"

"No." Sean laughs and rolls his eyes. Tom notes the lean jawline and the wry lips when they smile. "At night. You get out of bed and can go all night and nothing looks different. Masses tossing away millions. Day and night. The lights are always on, and it always looks the same. It's just a little cooler at night."

"I think you're tired right now."

"Yeah, but what're you gonna do about it? Gonna tuck me in?"

"If I knew your room number, maybe I would."

Sean laughs and nods his head down, his eyes closing a bit and resembling an old man. He opens his eyes and, as if it were a cup of Colombian Supremo, downs the rest of his drink. He waves emphatically to the waitress to get another one.

"So you're never going to have to work again," Sean says.

"I told you I've made my decision. It was a mistake to begin with."

"Who? Tom Ledger. *The* Tom Ledger making a mistake? Not him." Sean is shouting.

"Pipe down."

"Aw, shut up. You can't tell me what to do."

"So, am I staying with you tonight?"

Sean nods.

"Can you walk me there?"

"Let's go out."

"We are out," Tom says.

"No, I mean to a club."

"No, that's quite all right."

"I'm dating a chick over at the Wild Hare. It's within

walking distance."

"Not tonight. You need some rest."

"I'm not that bad. Man—it really has been—"

"You're falling asleep in midsentence, Sean."

"It's been a long—"

"A long what?" Tom asks.

Sean glances at Tom and grins, showing white teeth that Tom remembers in braces.

"Been a long time. Too long. You should come around more often."

They walk through the casino, past swarming crowds of men and women, all strangers in a foreign city. At close to one in the morning, their faces are long and lost, revealing little. Somebody hands Tom a flyer featuring half-naked women and bright phone numbers pictured in bold. Cars and taxis pass, and the sea of life seems to surge and subside.

Tom thinks of the previous night, of the thousands of stars he admired out on the deck, and knows he couldn't be farther away from Dale and Lily's. It was hard to leave them again, and he promised to see them soon. He knows he will keep this promise. Whatever happens, he knows things are different now.

Sean staggers, and Tom helps his brother balance as they walk the blocks toward the Mirage.

"Come on, man. The Wild Hare. We don't have to pay a cover charge."

"I don't think so," Tom says.

Sean pleads a little while longer and then forgets what he's talking about. They arrive at the Mirage, and Sean gives him the room number. It takes them a few minutes to ride the elevator to the thirty-second floor.

Sean guides Tom down a hallway to his door.

"Home sweet home," Sean says with a laugh.

Tom swipes the key card to open the ordinary-sized hotel room, which looks like it's been trashed by a rock group staying there for a month.

"Pardon the mess," Sean says, sweeping a pile of clothes and an open, empty suitcase off one of the two queen beds in the room, then falling backward onto the bed.

The tall, skinny body resting like a corpse in its deathbed triggers pity inside of Tom. It also produces a groundswell of guilt. Tom knows he's helpless against the guilt if he doesn't put it to rest right away.

Tom sits on a chair next to a desk littered with bills and random pieces of mail. He spots a corner of what looks like a check and wonders if it's his brother's paycheck, but he doesn't brave looking at the figure. Instead, he looks around the room, which is pretty much standard issue. An armoire holds a twenty-seven-inch Sony. On the knee-high cabinet to its left rests an assorted still life: two extra cartons of Marlboro Lights, a quarter-full bottle of Tanqueray gin, an empty hotel glass and another one full of soggy butts, several empty soda cans.

Tom thinks of getting himself another room for a night. Give his brother—or maybe himself—some privacy. He decides to write a note and opens the desk drawer for the routine hotel letterhead they usually put in a folder full of the hotel information and room service. All he finds in the drawer is a Bible, one of those Gideon kinds that turn up everywhere.

He picks up the Bible and opens it, remembering something his uncle told him. Psalm. Or Psalms. He spends a few minutes thumbing through the pages, looking mostly near the back until he eventually stumbles upon the book of Psalms close to the middle. The verse or chapter his uncle mentioned doesn't come to mind until he remembers what floor they're on. Thirty-two.

He finds the Thirty-second Psalm and starts to read.

"Blessed is he whose transgression is forgiven, whose sin is covered. Blessed is the man—"

Tom closes the Gideon Bible and puts it back in the desk drawer.

Forgiven transgressions and covered sins. Whatever.

He knows the drill, the supposed way it works. You read the Bible, the what—what is it called? The Holy Word? God's Word? Something about a Word. You read it and then what—you're saved? He vaguely remembers that when Billy Graham talks about salvation, everyone sings a song and about half the audience walks down to the front, where people look like they're handing out candy or money or something. Goodness knows something needs to be in the front for all those people to go down there.

But there's nothing like that in this hotel room. No music. No preacher. And this Word—this stuff about transgressions and being blessed—isn't ringing any bells.

Tom glances at Sean's mouth, half open, breathing silently.

Blessed is the man who has a screwup for a brother, for he will always know better.

He can't stop staring at Sean. This kid in a man's body and clothing. This youngster living alone in this pit of a home.

What if I never told him I love him, he wonders.

157

He wonders if he does actually love his brother. Sure, he's come to see him, but only after he almost died. Is that what love is?

You almost die, and then you suddenly get a case of the Mister Rogers syndrome, where you suddenly want every day to be a beautiful day in the neighborhood.

But Tom knows he loves Sean and always has, in his own way.

Just like Pop, right?

The thought angers Tom. He pushes it away.

You're no better than he was. You're no better than this alcoholic kid either.

He walks over and pours himself a glass of gin, emptying the bottle. He downs it and winces and swallows hard and hates the wretched taste in his mouth.

You're all alike.

When they moved to Colorado after their father's death, Tom dealt with the change the only way he knew how—with anger and silence. Sean and his outgoing, sensitive, questioning, incredibly likable personality always annoyed Tom. So Tom managed to always have somewhere to go, someone to meet, something to do— all as far from Sean as he could get. After the move, Tom became his own boss, knowing what he wanted to be and do. Sean simply got lost, and now, so many years later, he was still unfound.

"I'm sorry," Tom says to his little brother.

He wishes Sean can hear him.

❖ ❖ ❖

The whirl of electronic beeps and clinks fills the room as he walks toward the elevator. A woman in heels and a long coat covering what appears to be a fancy teddy walks by him and shines red lips. Tom wonders if they serve drinks here at ten in the morning. He wonders if his brother would rather have a drink instead of the coffee he's bringing him.

When he left him an hour ago, Sean still lay in the same pose as the night before: chest forward, arms slightly above his head, his face resting on one side, the mouth open enough to leak a small puddle on the sheet underneath. Same clothes, same everything, as though ten minutes instead of a whole night had passed.

Tom can't believe the crowd already assembled in the slots area of the Mirage. Feeding it in, pulling it back, waiting for something to register. Feeding, pulling, waiting. Again and again. Occasionally hearing something, unfazed, wanting more, wanting something magical to happen, some light to begin to turn into a siren and everything to stop and their life to take a turn for the better. Tom pities the poor fools bound by their petty hopes.

He thinks about his cell phone, which is off, and remembers the gamble he made with Sloan. The bet. Take something and turn it around and have his dreams answered just like that. As easily as slipping in a token and winning the big one.

That is what he wanted. The big one. Until a detour hit him.

Tom steps on the elevator and waits until the doors open for the thirty-second floor. He walks back to the room and wonders if Sean experiences hangovers or if he's beyond those. The card key is in his shirt pocket, and he takes it out and slips it in, holding Sean's coffee in the other hand. He opens the door and sees a figure standing.

"You a coffee drinker?"

The man he tells this to is balding, with just a little hair on the two sides of his head. He smirks at Tom as he takes the cigarette out of his mouth.

"Love the stuff," says the mustached man wearing a dress shirt and slacks.

In a second Tom has seen enough. The bald man standing, the other sitting in the same chair Tom sat in last night, and his brother, sitting on the edge of the bed. Wide awake, eyes pleading with Tom.

"Sean—"

"Tom, I'm sorry, man."

Tom stares at his brother and doesn't understand.

"I told them you'd talk to them," Sean says.

Tom stands still, the door behind him already shut.

"What are you talking about?" he asks his brother.

"Your little brother helped us out, Mr. Ledger," the

bald man says in an almost sarcastic, late-night-host sort of tone.

"Helped how?"

"You're here, aren't you? Just like he said."

Tom opens his mouth to say something, then sees his brother holding a half glass of something clear.

Must've had something else stashed somewhere.

"Morning cocktail there?" Tom asks.

"Look, man, just sit and listen to them," Sean says. "All right?"

Tom nods and looks over at the medium-built man who faces him. He opens the top to the coffee and then launches the cup in the man's face, catching him just as he opens up his mouth to hurtle an order that soon becomes a scream.

Before the man even stops yelling, Tom is out of the room, sprinting down the carpeted hallway toward the elevator. Steps pound after him, a voice, several curses, and the pleading and desperate words yelled by his brother.

"What are you doing, Tom? Come on, man! Come back here!"

The elevator button lights up as Tom puts his whole fist against it. He hears steps and looks down the hallway to see the mustached man, younger and more fit than the bald one, jogging down the hall. Tom gives up on the elevators and runs in the opposite direction. He turns left and gallops down the next lengthy hallway, eventually turning again and coming upon another elevator.

He presses the button and waits. Waits. His heart pounding, his head moving in order to somehow make the elevator go faster. Waits. Then sprints off again, knowing he's waited too long.

He turns another corner and runs into a maid's cart, turning it over and strewing a week's worth of soaps and shampoos onto the carpet. No one is around to see his mishap. Scrambling to his feet, he darts down the hallway and nears another elevator. As if on cue, the door opens up. He looks back down the hallway and sees Sean's skinny figure staring at him in complete confusion and even a bit of amusement. Tom passed by the room again without even noticing.

They stare at one another for a fraction of a second before Tom steps onto the elevator and presses the button for the lobby.

Perhaps there should be a dramatic chase all over the hotel with men carrying Uzis and speaking foreign dialects racing up and down the stairs. But these are businessmen Tom is dealing with. Men used to shouting orders and getting results by simply waving a boss's authority in front of someone's face. Tom walks out of the casino and takes a cab to the parking lot where he left his car.

Sean.

Something tells him to go back, to make sure Sean is okay. But he saw everything he needed to see. Sean telling him everything's cool, everything's gonna be fine. Sean drinking casually as if these two men were old buddies.

Did Sean call them? Did they call him? How did Sloan know about Sean? How could he know Sean was staying in a hotel room, of all things.

In the backseat of the cab, Tom puts a hand to his side and realizes his phone is missing. It's where he left it, on the table next to the good ol' Gideon Bible and a glass that smells like gin.

It's Tom."

"Tom who?"

He pauses, then speaks clearly into the pay phone.

"Allegra, it's me."

"Okay," she replies after a pause. Too long of a pause.

"I need to see you."

He waits to hear her response, if there is one. He knows he can only expect the inevitable. He deserves anything she might dish out and then some. Tom knows this now.

"What's wrong?" Allegra asks him.

"Everything. But nothing serious. I mean, no one died or anything like that. Something happened. I need to talk to you."

"You are talking to me."

Her voice is terse, mature. It could almost belong to a stranger.

Maybe it does.

"I need to talk to you in person."

"Really? Where are you calling from?"

"Room 894."

She makes a sound, stopping herself on the first syllable, then pauses again.

"Is this a joke?"

"I checked in last night," Tom replies.

"Checked in."

"I'm at the Hideaway."

"Where—"

"Aunt Lily."

"She told you where I work?"

"Yes."

"I'm surprised you even asked."

The sound of Allegra's voice after so long seems unreal, as if it belonged in a dream. So many years, and the same confident yet soft voice is in his ear.

"I know. It's been a long time."

"It's been longer than that, Tom. You must know that too."

"Could I talk with you face-to-face?"

It's a question he knows she can only say yes to. Five minutes away, at the most—that's how far he is from Allegra right now. Even if she refuses, he can run down to the lobby and find her just as she begins to sneak away from the guest-relations desk she sits behind.

What does she look like? Now. Today. Is it even close to the beauty portrayed on the picture sent to his aunt and uncle?

Tom knows the answer. He just wants to see for himself. See a face he's imagined for years, see a face memorized in that one simple photo he kept for some reason.

"I get off work in half an hour."

"I know," Tom says.

"Checked it out already?" She chuckles. "Some

165

things never change."

"Maybe. But sometimes situations do."

"You don't say?"

He is unsure what she means as she tells him she'll be waiting by the west-side pool. Tom hangs up the phone, leans back on the bed, and closes his eyes.

❖   ❖   ❖

There is a dock stretching out into the Pacific somewhere off Coastal Drive. Tom took Allegra there one Saturday to tell her good-bye, and even there he never told her the truth. In all their time together, he never told her the honest and legitimate truth she so deserved.

Perhaps she was better off, Tom thinks, wondering. *Maybe in the long run, she got the better end of the deal.*

It happened after lunch, after Allegra asked Tom what was wrong. Tom never opened up to her, never told her his feelings about work and how much he hated it, how much he hated himself for being stuck in a going-nowhere career. Tom tried to pour these insecure feelings into the work itself, making Allegra think he was simply overworked and underpaid and always tired.

Tom said nothing over his picked-at sandwich. They strolled out to the pier, which was half-full with a combination of locals and tourists enjoying the extended summer of September. Allegra reached for Tom's hand but he slid it away.

They reached the end of the pier, and Allegra had turned to walk back when Tom stopped her.

"Allie. We have to talk."

Allegra's smooth skin glowed warm in the sun and

her sunglasses reflected Tom's face. She wore a white tank top with her black hair dipping over a lean shoulder. Long legs filled in white shorts.

"Okay."

Her voice mirrored the day. Breezy and calm, almost soothing.

"This trip I'm going on . . ."

She looked at him and waited.

"Yeah?" she finally asked.

"I'm not coming back."

And with those words, he said good-bye. There was no drama, no argument or harsh words. Allegra wasn't like that. Tom was thankful for her sunglasses, which must have shielded shell-shocked eyes. Instead, he simply saw the lines of tears running down her cheeks, leaking from beneath the shaded securities. They talked for a while, and Allegra asked why.

"I need to get away from all of this."

"From all of what?" Allegra asked him.

"I quit my job a week ago."

"Were you going to tell me?"

"I just did," he said.

"So 'all of this'—what is that supposed to mean? California? The ocean? Your job?"

"Everything."

"Everything. Even me?"

He nodded. Thinking back on this years later, moments before he is about to see Allegra for the first time after so many years, he realizes the absolute gall it took for him to nod at her when she asked that. The woman he shared a home with, the woman he shared a bed with, the woman he shared a life with—he was rejecting her with an arrogant dip of the head, lumping her in with a job he hated and a state where he'd been a failure.

Allegra acted composed as they walked back to the apartment. But inside—what was going on inside? What kind of agony did those shiny sunglasses hide?

I don't deserve to even see her, Tom thinks. *I don't have the right to be here.*

He simply nodded. And eventually he left. Never telling her the truth. Never once telling her how much he loved her. Never telling her that he didn't know how capable a man like him was of loving anyone or just what that love was comprised of.

Did love mean leaving her with a simple nod? Was that the only kind of love Tom was capable of?

Years later, Tom believes that it was. Still is, to this day. And he is glad, in a sense, that he never told Allegra the full truth. That he believed there could never be another woman like her, that he had fallen in love with her and that love scared him more than anything. It would have sounded like a cliché. A cop-out.

It was a cop-out, a voice tells him. *It was a cop-out just like your thirty-four years have been. Just like the fact that you walked away from that plane crash while the man sitting beside you who probably knew the true meaning of the word* love *ended up dying.*

Tom remembers Allegra's grace and dignity, the fact that she continued to walk back with him to their apartment that day, the fact that she still reached for his hand on the way back, the fact that she obviously still loved him.

He wonders if there is any portion of that love still inside of her.

Even in a khaki skirt and a regulation Hideaway Cove hotel polo shirt, Allegra makes an impression on the pool patrons. She wears brown leather sandals with just a hint of a heel, and as she nears Tom he notices a thin gold anklet around one of those honey-colored legs. Still fit and trim, with a figure many of the poolside men would love to see sunbathing next to them, Allegra wears small sunglasses, which she takes off as she nears his chair. She doesn't smile when she sees him.

"I almost went home for the day," she says, fifteen minutes later than her originally suggested time.

"I could have gone there."

"What do you want?"

Cold, almost ruthless eyes glare at him. The fact that they're so exotic and he remembers them lit up with a smile makes them all the more startling.

Tom stands by the chair. At first he wasn't sure whether to hug or kiss her. Now he wonders if she'll suddenly try to pummel him.

"Allegra, something happened to me recently."

"Are you broke?" she asks.

Tom can't help staring at the lips he's kissed a thousand times. Maybe even more. Curvy, full lips that one can't help notice.

"No."

"Dale and Lily—?"

"Are fine. Everyone's fine. Well, Sean doesn't count. He's not so hot."

"You saw Sean?"

Tom nods.

"When?"

"Just came from visiting him."

Her look reveals surprise and alarm at the same time. They both continue to stand at an awkward distance, neither seeming to want to budge an inch.

"Look, could we sit down or something? Maybe go up to the restaurant and grab a table?"

"Need a drink?" she asks.

"I never did."

"People change," Allegra says.

"Have you?"

She flips hair that is slightly shorter than he remembers it. Shorter than the Christmas picture. "More than you know."

Allegra leads him around the pool and greets the people she passes, even remembering a couple of names. They reach wooden steps that climb to a wooden deck set right off of the restaurant and bar. Several people sit in barstools at the round tables finishing lunch.

"I can get you a free lunch," Allegra says. "Only this once."

She still hasn't given him the hint of a smile.

"I know this is awkward."

"There's nothing *awkward* about this, Tom."

"You know what I mean."

"No, I don't think I do. What are you doing here?"

He wants to tell her to stop being so cold and angry, to simply smile for a moment and actually greet him. They once were lovers.

"The plane that went down in Nebraska last week. I was on that flight."

She blinks hard and then stares at him to study his face and see if he's lying. Her cheeks draw in slightly, and she looks away. A tear wells up in one eye.

"Are you serious?"

He nods. "I got out with just a cut lip. A lot of people died in the crash, but for some reason, I walked away."

Allegra puts a hand over her mouth, still looking away.

"Allegra—" he begins.

That same hand goes in the air, waving him off, telling him to be quiet for a minute. Her composure, her self-assurance, and her cold anger all dissolve as tears form in her eyes and she begins to cry.

"Excuse me," she says, getting up and hurrying away into the restaurant. In the meantime, a waiter asks Tom what he wants.

"Nothing, now. Maybe just a lemonade or something like that."

He waits for a few moments, and Allegra walks back out, the tears in her eyes gone but in their place a heavy shadow.

"I'm sorry," Allegra says.

"No, *I'm* sorry. Allegra—"

Tom unexpectedly reaches out and takes her hand.

"Allegra, there are so many things I know I need to

say. I'm sitting across from you like it's nothing and yet—it's been so many years. I can't apologize—nothing could ever make up—I just—something awful happened and I needed to see you."

"Are you okay?" her voice asks, the same voice from yesteryear, the same tone that used to whisper good night in his ear after they turned the lights off.

"Yes. I think so. I don't know. Ever since I got off the plane, everything in my life's been a little—nothing's been the same."

"Did you tell your uncle and aunt?"

He nods. "It was good to see them, but they—I don't know, they turned the whole thing into a religious experience. And that's not really what's happening with me. At least I don't think so. I just know something's different. And I haven't been able to stop thinking about you. I've wanted to tell you about it. I've wanted to sit and see you and hear your voice."

He brushes back his hair and realizes he's still holding her hand. He lets go.

"I—I know I don't have any business coming back here. I don't have a right. I just—there was nowhere else I could imagine going. No one else I wanted to be with."

"What about back in Chicago?"

He shakes his head. "No one. No one that would have cared."

Heartfelt, hurting eyes lock onto his own. She shakes her head, saying so much by not saying anything.

"Can I just—just for a while, even just an hour or two—can I just be with you? Just know you're there, sitting across from me?"

Allegra motions her head yes.

"I've been here for a long time," she tells him.

❖   ❖   ❖

First he tells her about the accident, about meeting the man named Kent Marks and running through the fire and ending up in a cornfield. He tells her about visiting with his family and brother. He eventually stops himself, realizing he unleashed a geyser full of information over her.

"I shouldn't talk so much."

Allegra watches him in amazement.

"What?" Tom asks.

"I can't believe you're here."

"I know."

"How long has it been?" Allegra asks.

"At least six years."

A surge of guilt races through Tom like a drug.

"I know nothing can change those years, or what happened."

"I wouldn't change them if I could," Allegra says, surprising him.

"How long have you worked at this hotel?"

"Several years. It's a good job. They pay very well, have decent benefits. And days like today—I only have to work a morning shift from six to one."

"Do you live far from here?"

"In Del Ray. Just about fifteen minutes away. An apartment on the ocean."

"You always loved the ocean." Tom smiles.

"All you have is a big lake, right?"

"Yes. You wouldn't have been able to stand it."

173

"Someone never gave me the opportunity."

Tom looks down at the table and sees a ring he gave her years ago.

"Yes, I still wear it. Probably foolish, but I always loved it. Blue topaz is my favorite. Well, after diamonds, of course. But seeing as I won't be getting one of those anytime soon—"

That's the first thing she's revealed about herself. He keeps wanting to ask Allegra about her life. What does she do for fun? Does she date? Has she fallen in love since he left? How is her family? Yet each potential question fills him with shame, and he imagines her firing back sarcastic retorts that he would richly deserve. He doesn't want to argue with her. He doesn't want conflict. So he searches for an innocuous question.

"Do you see yourself staying here for a while?"

"In California?" Allegra asks.

"No. I mean, here, at the hotel."

"I think so. Probably."

He nods.

"What about you?" she asks.

"What do you mean?"

"Are you in California for long?"

"Sure. I think. I don't know." He sighs. "There's a lot in my life I've got to reevaluate."

"Listen, I probably should get home," Allegra tells him, urgency in her voice.

Disappointment creeps in. Tom hoped he could be with her this evening and tonight. Nothing happening. Just talking. Just reconnecting. Just knowing she's there.

She must have seen it on his face. "Maybe we could see each other tomorrow."

"I'm staying overnight here, so that might be a possibility."

"I'm off tomorrow," Allegra replies.

"Oh."

She seems nervous. He can't tell if she's brushing him off. "I'd prefer to get away from here. Maybe we could go somewhere."

"Okay," he says.

She stands, directing her guarded smile toward him. Eyes that change color in the sunlight, a lighter green now as she stares down at him, remind him of a thousand days when he gazed into them and never tiring of their allure.

"Maybe you could even come over to the apartment," Allegra replies with a bit of reserve, almost hesitation.

"It's—whatever. I didn't come here—I don't expect—"

"It's fine," her composed voice tells him. "I'm really glad you came."

He nods and watches her glide away and wonders how six years truly could have passed and how he could have overlooked her all that time.

❖   ❖   ❖

The hotel consists of four different buildings with doors that open either toward the plush, tropical landscape in front or the large pools in back. The rooms have a veranda feel, with large interiors that likely accommodate as many newlyweds as business travelers. Tom feels strange relaxing on the down comforter, feeling as though he should do something. But there's nothing he wants to do. Except see Allegra, which he can't do until tomorrow.

He watches a game on ESPN, dozes for a while, gets up and brushes his teeth. Finally he leaves his room and walks down to the swimming pool located just beyond the palm trees and bushes. A mock bonfire has been set up on one side of the cleared patio, and a group of about thirty business-casual-dressed people mingle nearby. Tables are set for a buffet-style dinner. An open bar is set up near a flowering hedge, the bartender grinning as he serves the crowd.

High laughter and glassy eyes greet Tom as he nears the reception. Undaunted, he walks up to the bartender and orders a gin and tonic. The first sip tastes good. Tom carries the drink through the crowd and goes to sit down on the edge of a plastic lounge chair. He watches the flames from several torches throw flickering waves of orange over the crowd. Tom sips his drink and watches the people.

He's been to many of these functions before. Business events. Corporate functions where they fly a group of twenty or thirty people out and leave them unattended during the night after a long day of boring conferences. The companies provide free luxury room and board and complimentary food and beverages. All you can eat and drink and whatever you want to do—including getting plastered and insulting the boss or making a move on a colleague's wife. Tom's seen many careers ended because of functions like the one he's watching.

I left her for this, Tom realizes with shame. *I left Allegra to have a life full of this.*

Meaningless relationships. Climbing the corporate ladder. Brownnosing. Backstabbing. Greed. Suits and ties and heels and briefcases and laptops and spreadsheets—it's all enough to make him want to throw up. Six years later, Tom sees clearly that he made a big mistake. Not in pursuing business, but in pursuing it apart from Allegra.

He thinks of her comment when he told her she wouldn't like Lake Michigan.

"Someone never gave me the opportunity."

He left without a second thought. And a second thought never came to him, not in all that long time. There were days when he hated the job, hated the people around him, hated what he was slowly becoming. But Tom never woke up hating *himself.* Perhaps that's who he should have hated all along.

Another sip. As he peers into his glass, a figure blocks the light on his right.

"Need a refill there?"

His eyes glimpse heels and long, tanned legs that end in a black skirt just above well-toned knees. A silky white tank top rounds off the outfit, and for just the briefest of seconds, Tom believes and *knows* that it is Allegra coming to him tonight, coming back here again. Then his eyes reach the woman's face and take in the chin-length blonde hair.

"I saw you slip through the crowd," she tells him, smiling brilliantly white teeth. "You're not at this conference, are you?"

Tom shakes his head.

"Can I get you another?" she asks him again.

"Aren't I supposed to ask you that?"

"Not necessarily. It's not like buying me a drink. They're free."

"I'm good, thanks."

She steps closer to him. "What's your name?"

Her eyes are as bold as she is. In the flickering light she looks like a glamorous movie star sliding up to talk with him. They are far enough away from the main crowd to not be heard or noticed.

"Tom."

"I'm Tricia."

He nods again, feeling her interest and the familiar thrill it gave him. This was always his weakness. Not the drinking, not the corporate politics, but giving in to a beautiful face and body whenever he got the chance. Being alone and single, he could do things like that. He could do what he wanted to.

Maybe it's time to do it again.

He hears a high-pitched voice talking to him, doesn't hear the words she's speaking. But then he never heard their words, and he always disregarded their looks afterward. No one ever touched him deep inside except for one time and one time only.

Allegra was different. She is different. And no matter how many years go by, how many women he dates to escape her memory, how much money and wealth he might accumulate, nothing, absolutely nothing, will take away this longing deep inside.

"I'm sorry," Tom says, standing.

"What?" Tricia asks, giving him a confused smile.

"I've got to go."

"Where do you want to go?"

"Away from here."

"I can—do you want me to come with?"

He stares at her and knows it's the liquor talking. Liquor and insecurity. She'll regret it the next day, but it doesn't matter right now. The moment is always now. That's the way it is with almost everyone. They live for the moment and want what's best for themselves and never think of tomorrow and never question the consequences.

Everyone always expects to wake up and find a brighter, happier day. No one ever expects the plane to crash.

"No, thanks," Tom says. "Nice to meet you."

He leaves Tricia and the party behind and strolls around the hotel grounds for a few minutes. He wants to call Allegra, wants to be near her. Seeing her today—it couldn't have been six years since he last saw her, could it?

If I die in my sleep tonight, what would I have wanted to do or say?

What if there is no tomorrow?

What if I only have one more chance?

Tom finds his way through the main lobby of the south building and back to his room and knows he must call Allegra. His watch says nine-thirty, so he knows it's early enough.

What if she doesn't want to talk with him? What if she's changed her mind about seeing him tomorrow?

I didn't come halfway across the country to not even try.

He calls her number. A voice answers on the third ring.

"Hello?"

It's her. Not another voice. Not a male voice. It's Allegra.

"I couldn't wait till tomorrow."

A pause.

"I'm sorry for calling. I just—all I'm doing is thinking of you."

"Tom—"

"Can I see you tonight?"

"It wouldn't be a good idea."

"I know it wouldn't. I know I don't deserve to even talk to you. Allegra, I'm realizing what I've done."

"Tom, please."

"Can we just talk?"

He knows he sounds desperate. He is. He's sadly desperate and feels a void he's never felt before. He doesn't want to be alone anymore.

"Not tonight."

"I don't have to come over. We can just talk like this, on the phone."

"I can't," Allegra says, her voice frustrated.

"Why not?"

"Tom, someone's here."

He stops, his heart bursting, his fears answered.

"Someone?"

"I can tell you about it tomorrow."

"What do you mean?"

"Tom, not now. Not like this."

Just after she says that, she muffles the phone, putting a hand over the receiver, and Tom can hear a tiny bit of conversation. She uncovers the phone again.

"Please, Tom. I have to go."

"Yeah, okay. I'm sorry."

"No, I just—tomorrow. Call me in the morning."

"Will you be alone?" he asks.

"I can meet you somewhere," she answers, avoiding his question.

Tom hangs up and realizes that he is indeed alone. He left Allegra six years ago without a second thought, knowing she would find another. Someone as beautiful and as amazing as Allegra would easily find someone else. He's surprised she isn't married with a family by now.

I chose this life, Tom knows. *I made the mistake.*

He takes off his shirt and sits on the chair in his slacks, staring at the change and the rental car keys on the table. His wallet sits next to them, a wallet containing the last shreds of his former life—including, he assumes, the memory stick with the information he stole from Hammett-Korning. He hasn't even cared to check on it the last few days.

On the chair across from his is the bag Earl gave him. There is still a T-shirt in there Tom hasn't worn. The only other thing apart from a warm bottled water and a few candy bars is the Bible Earl gave him.

He takes the Bible out and opens it up—anything to take his mind off Allegra. He again tries the psalm he was told to read. This version sounds a little different as he begins to read Psalm 32:

> What happiness for those whose guilt has been forgiven! What joys when sins are covered over! What relief for those who have confessed their sins and God has cleared their record.

Tom snorts at this last phrase, this business about God clearing records. What if the record is long and full of a hundred, maybe even a thousand wrongs. Sins. Bad things. Whatever they might be called. Things Tom has done that he shouldn't have done.

Would God ever clear up his record with women? What about his dismal record with Allegra?

> There was a time when I wouldn't admit what a sinner I was. But my dishonesty made me miserable and filled my days with frustration. All day and all night your hand was heavy on me. My strength evaporated like water on a sunny day until I finally admitted all my sins to you and stopped trying to hide them. I said to myself, "I will confess them to the Lord." And you forgave me! All my guilt is gone.

Stop this, Tom tells himself. *Stop reading.*

> Now I say that each believer should confess his sins to God when he is aware of them, while there is time to be

182

forgiven. Judgment will not touch him if he does.

This is ludicrous. And the fact that you're reading it, that you're actually reading it and even mildly thinking that it could be true or real—-come on, man. Get a grip.

You are my hiding place from every storm of life; you even keep me from getting into trouble! You surround me with songs of victory. I will instruct you (says the Lord) and guide you along the best pathway for your life; I will advise you and watch your progress. Don't be like a senseless horse or mule that has to have a bit in its mouth to keep it in line!

Tom stops before finishing the passage. He wipes a tear out of one corner of his eye and shakes his head. He laughs. This is all just way too much. This really must be post-traumatic syndrome he's going through. He almost dies in a plane accident and suddenly he becomes this sickening, gooey pale image of a man who's wallowing in the past and getting weepy over Bible verses.

Mules and bits in the mouth are nothing but nonsense.

Yet he knows that the tear does make sense. And the words actually seem clear to him. Perfectly clear.

Many sorrows come to the wicked, but abiding love surrounds those who trust in the Lord. So rejoice in him, all those who are his, and shout for joy, all those who try to obey him.

Tom wonders who wrote that passage so many years

ago. What sort of guilt did he suffer? Surely it couldn't be as bad as his own. Maybe this man did something bad, but what about leaving the love of your life behind without a shred of guilt or a hint of doubt? What about thirty-four years of living for yourself and only for yourself and needing a plane disaster to somehow get your attention?

What about an entire life full of me?

He reads the verse again.

"There was a time when I wouldn't admit what a sinner I was. But my dishonesty made me miserable and filled my days with frustration." He skips ahead. "I said to myself, 'I will confess them to the Lord.' And you forgave me! All my guilt is gone."

Could my guilt really be gone? Like this writer says? Did someone truly feel guilt when he wrote this and then was truly forgiven?

Tom knows he could confess his sins and his guilt. He could begin writing down all the ways he has messed up his life. He could put them all down or say them out loud. But he can't see what good that will do him.

I wish I could talk to Kent Marks again, he thinks. *I wish I could ask him these questions. I wish I could know who wrote this and whether it actually was real.*

Tom closes the Bible and tells himself to turn on the television and try to sleep. Tomorrow, if it decides to come, will be a brand-new day. Tomorrow might offer him more hope than tonight does.

He stares at the end of a baseball game with a thought rolling over in his head. Something he just read.

A hiding place from every storm of life.

He would give almost anything for that hiding place.

He only wonders if it's truly out there for him to find.

❖ ❖ ❖

The stairs creak out their age as Tom ascends them. Black-and-white photos of quaint Italian scenes decorate the stark white of the wall he passes. The aroma of fresh basil and garlic makes him realize how little he's eaten over the last few days. He reaches the top and looks around the compact dining room. In one corner, Allegra sits alone, waiting for him.

He walks over to her and notices there are only two other people in the restaurant, though it's only a little past noon.

"I took a couple of wrong turns," Tom says, sitting down in a chair next to hers.

"You haven't been around here for a while, have you?" Allegra asks.

He shakes his head as he marvels at Allegra's beauty. Her skin is flawless, with just enough makeup around her eyes and lips. Her hair is tied back, and she wears a black, form-fitting tank top with jeans. Tom admires her long, lithe arms as she brings a wine glass up and takes a sip.

"I thought I might need this," Allegra says.

The waiter comes, and Tom orders a glass of the

house wine. They listen to the man as he lists off the specials, their eyes converging several times. After he leaves, they remain silent. Tom is not sure where to start.

"Thanks for meeting me here," he says.

Allegra nods and looks down at the skirted table.

"I don't know what to say. How to start out."

"Tell me about yourself. About your life."

"You really want to know?"

"Yes. Let's don't talk about the past."

Tom wrinkles his eyebrows in confusion. "I'm not sure how I can avoid it."

"Just don't mention it."

"But that's why I'm here."

"We can do that later. But just now, in this place, let's act like we've never been here before. Like it's a first date. Give ourselves a break."

Her eyes compel him to comply. He wonders how many tears those loving eyes have cried over the years, tears caused by his departure. He wonders if those eyes now belong to someone else. But these are things he cannot talk about now, cannot ask.

The glass of Chardonnay arrives, and Tom takes a sip.

"Are you ready to order?" the Italian waiter, probably the owner's son, asks them.

"Just a few more minutes," Tom replies. "So, Allegra Davi, what sort of food do you like?"

"I like Italian a lot."

Tom smiles, knowing it's her favorite and that she always gets either the baked ziti with meat sauce or the chicken parmesan. When they were together, they used to love coming to this tiny nook of a restaurant. It's still here, still called Cantera's years later.

"So are you one of those picky eaters? Are you adventurous in what you eat?"

She smiles a natural, no-baggage-attached grin. "I'm quite adventurous."

Every sentence brings a hundred memories to pick from, every topic a dozen connotations. Tom forces himself not to bring them up, not to reminisce.

"And what about you? Are you adventurous?"

"I'm not big on squishy things," he replies. "But I do like chicken parmesan."

"Me too."

"Wow," Tom says in jest. "The things you learn about a person."

"And I see you like Chardonnay?"

"I'm actually not a big drinker. Yourself?"

"Hardly ever," she says. "This is probably the first glass of wine I've had in a couple of years."

"Interesting. Did you feel it might help out during this—this first date?"

"Possibly." Again, Allegra can't contain her smile.

The waiter comes, and they order lunch, with Tom ordering the parmesan and Allegra ordering the ziti. When they are alone again, Allegra's face turns to him with a playful beam.

"So, Mr. Ledger, why did you want to ask me out today? What prompted you to after all this time?"

Tom is unsure how to answer this. He doesn't want to play this game the whole time they're here. He wants to comply with her wishes, but he also wants to do what he can to make up for the lost years. He is unsure where she stands with him.

"I remembered this remarkable woman I used to

187

know. I remembered the greatest thing that ever happened to me."

Her face suddenly somber, Allegra looks down at the table.

"Allegra, I need to talk with you. To really talk with you."

"I know. But not now. Not this instant."

"Why?"

"I don't want to ruin this. I don't want to ruin our lunch."

"We can always have a lunch," Tom says.

She shakes her head. "Tom, you don't understand. So much has changed. It's not like you can whisk in here and simply start over again."

"I'm not saying I can, Allie. I'm just—I want to know if there is any way I can somehow be a part of your life again."

"You're still part of my life, Tom. You've been a part of my life every day. You always will be."

Tom opens his mouth to say something, to ask for more of an explanation, to begin to try to tell her just how ignorant and selfish he's been over these years, but she moves a hand over and places it on top of his and simply shushes him.

"Let's enjoy this lunch. Please? No tension or conflict. Not now."

Tom nods, and she puts back on the playful expression.

"I have to say, you're still as handsome as you always were."

Tom chuckles. "Kind of rumpled, though. I've been living out of a bag for the last few days."

"So where are your belongings? Your clothes and furniture?"

"Still in Chicago. Ready to be moved."

"And you were moving here?"

"Let's pretend I'm living here. Just for the moment."

"Then how do you explain getting lost on the way here?" Allegra asks with a spark in her eyes.

"I've been lost for a long time. Longer than I realized."

❖   ❖   ❖

For two and a half hours, over a meal of crusty bread and Caesar salads and pasta, along with several glasses of wine, Tom and Allegra reconnect. While it's impossible for either not to go back in time, occasionally mentioning a memory or a connection to the days when they loved one another and were linked together in a hundred different ways, they also tell about their current lives. But Tom says relatively little about his work and his life in Chicago, having wanted to leave it behind for so long. He keeps steering the conversation back to Allegra's.

As they prepare to leave and Tom grabs the check, he finally comes right out and asks.

"So, there's no one else?"

Allegra groans. "Ah, the inevitable question."

"I can't help it."

"I could ask the same of you."

"The answer is no."

"So you've been a single man for the last few years."

"I've dated. But I've never gotten serious."

Allegra smiles. "I guess I could say the same."

"Really?"

"Yes."

They walk down the stairs and outside to the crystalline day. Across the street from the small house that contains Cantera's, apartments line the oceanfront.

"Want to take a walk?" Allegra asks.

"I probably need to."

They walk across the street and step up on a sidewalk in front of the apartment buildings. Allegra puts on her sunglasses and examines Tom. Then she surprises him by taking his hand.

"Lunch was wonderful, Tom," she says. "Thank you."

He looks down at her and sees her supple lips extend him a generous smile.

"Yeah, I enjoyed it too."

They begin to walk down the sidewalk.

"There's something I should tell you. I didn't know if I should. But, well—"

"What is it?" he asks.

"Remember when you asked if there's someone else in my life right now? Well there is."

Tom's heart sinks. He wonders if she is married, though he doubts it. He's pretty sure Allegra would have told him—or Aunt Lily and Uncle Dale would. But someone else? A casual boyfriend? A lover?

"How long have you been together?" Tom asks.

"For a while. Quite a while, actually."

Tom nods carefully.

"I could introduce you to him if you want."

"I don't know—do you really think that would be the best idea?"

He doesn't understand Allegra's tone, her hand in his, her warm smile, all while she's talking about another man in her life.

"Actually, I think it'd be great if you met him."

"I really *don't,*" Tom says.

Allegra stops in front of a cream-colored, three-story apartment building. On the top floor, a screen door slides open and a young woman steps out on the balcony, waving down at them.

"Hi, guys!" the college-aged blonde calls out.

Allegra waves back. Tom looks at her and then back at the stranger.

Then he sees the boy and suddenly understands. He wants to look at Allegra, to see her reaction, but he cannot take his eyes off the child who is waving down through the protective beams of the balcony.

"Hey, Mommy!" a little voice cries out, a little voice that moves Tom to open his mouth slightly and feel his heart rupture and wonder why he's lived an entire life for himself and himself only.

"Allegra?" he asks her.

"That's the man in my life." She still smiles, looking serene and controlled and still gloriously alluring. "Hi, Tommy."

The name answers his one and only question.

❖   ❖   ❖

A Polaroid moment he will carry to his grave. A single instance of surprise and humility and joy and sadness all compressed into the heart and soul of a little boy named Tommy. A few moments given to him from some unseen force, some higher power, some God he still doesn't believe in. After today, after this meeting, after this snapshot of surprise, Tom knows anything is possible.

Anything.

He climbs the apartment stairs after Allegra and sees the dark-haired boy rush over to greet his mother. Allegra acts relaxed and says a few words to the baby-sitter, a girl Allegra introduces but whom he instantly forgets after meeting her. He is entranced by the boy, this five-year-old life, this package of energy and splendor that he knows is his son.

Allegra tells Tommy to slow down for a moment and look at Tom.

"Tommy, there's someone I want you to meet. This man here is named Tom."

"I'm named Tom," his voice says.

Tom thinks it might be the most glorious voice he's ever heard.

He looks at Allegra and finds himself speechless. His gaze goes back down to Tommy.

His first words to his son—what will they be?

"I like your name," he says.

"Tell Mr. Tom how old you are," Allegra tells the boy with a handful of freckles on his nose.

"Five and a half."

Allegra and Tom share a glance, and he knows. Nothing more needs to be spoken or told. He feels as though he's in the plane again, spiraling down to earth, attempting to land, shaking and rocking. He readies himself and braces for impact and sees his life flash before his eyes and suddenly realizes all the things he should have done and didn't. It's the same feeling, yet worse.

The baby-sitter leaves, but Tom doesn't notice her departure. He bends down on his knees and stares at the kid, who is playing with some cars on the carpet of the family room. Tom hasn't noticed any of the decor of Allegra's home. He is utterly amazed at this youngster in front of him.

"What are you playing with?" his unsteady voice asks.

"These are my cars. Do you want to play?"

Tom nods and picks up a car and makes a noise and sees the boy studying him. Overwhelmed, Tom leans over and gives the boy a hug. Tears form at his eyes.

"Hey," Tommy protests. Tom lets him go to resume playing.

Tom stands up and looks at Allegra.

"I didn't know how to tell you," she says.

Tom wipes the tears from his eyes. "All this time."

She nods.

He finds a chair and sits down, watching his son.

Tommy plays diligently with his cars, creating lines of them and parking them and carefully driving them around one another. Tom notices that Tommy is dark from the beach but still is lighter-skinned than Allegra. His features echo both of them—the thick, straight black hair, which Allegra has cut short, the dark eyebrows, the green eyes. Tommy's nose is small and his long legs make him look tall. But Tom is unsure how tall five-year-olds usually are.

"Is he in school?"

"Not during the summer," Allegra says, sitting on the couch across from him.

"What grade is he?"

"He will be starting first grade in the fall. I put him in kindergarten early. He's really bright for his age."

I missed kindergarten, Tom thinks. *I missed his first day of school, his first parent-teacher conference, his first everything.*

I missed it and will never be able to get it back.

"How'd he do in kindergarten?"

"Very well. I think he takes after his father by being so smart."

"Why didn't you—" Tom begins, a tinge of anger rising in him.

"What? Contact you? Tell you?"

"No," he says, letting out a sigh. "I know."

"Do you? Do you remember the pier? What you said? What you *didn't* say?"

"I know."

Allegra speaks to him in a hushed tone.

"How could I expect to tell you? I didn't even know about Tommy until you were gone. And then I didn't know where you went. All you said was that it was over. Nothing more. How could I contact you?"

Tom looks at Tommy and sees him ignoring their conversation.

"I didn't mean—I shouldn't have said anything. You had every right never to tell me."

"I thought about it. I've thought about it for many years. I just—I was so hurt, Tom."

"I'm sorry," he says, wishing he could say or do something more.

"He's an incredible child. I'm thankful for him every day."

"Did you tell Lily and Dale?"

Allegra nods. This spites Tom even more—that his aunt and uncle knew and didn't tell him. Is he that selfish and awful a human not to have been told by his own flesh and blood?

"I asked them not to tell you."

"Have they met him?"

Allegra tells him yes.

This is too much. Everything now is too much.

"I don't know what to say."

"You don't have to say anything."

Tom looks at her, his jaw clenched and his hands clasping each other.

"How can I get back six years? How can I go and turn back time?"

"You can't."

"Yeah," he says in deep thought, searching for something right to say.

"Should I not have told you now?" Allegra asks.

"No, I'm glad you did. I just—"

An awful thought crosses his mind.

"What?"

"If I had died in the plane crash. If I hadn't walked away. I would have never—"

"But you did," Allegra says.

Tom suddenly understands Allegra's reaction yesterday when he told her about the accident.

Kent Marks knew his children. He was a father to them. But Tom didn't even know he had a son, and his son probably didn't know his father even existed. And Kent's God allowed *Tom* to live.

Why?

"Does he know?" Tom asks, looking at Tommy. "Does he know about his father?"

"I told him he left a long time ago, that it's just him and I."

"Has he ever seen pictures? I mean, would he know?"

Allegra shakes her head.

Tom wants to tell the boy the truth. That he's his father. That he's the one who left years ago. That he's sorry. That he loves him.

What if Allegra had told me shortly after I left her? Tom wonders. *What would I have done?*

Tom thinks he knows, and the truth is ugly. It's ugly just like his thirty-four years have been.

I've done absolutely nothing except live for myself.

He stares in silence at the little boy and his trucks. He's reminded of a verse from yesterday: "All my guilt is gone." But he knows there's an ocean of guilt sloshing around inside of him, vaster than the mighty Pacific.

"Tom, I didn't want to hurt you."

196

"I deserve to be hurt. To be hurt really bad."

"No you don't."

"I have no idea what to say or do now."

Tommy looks up at him and smiles, then resumes playing with the cars.

"You don't have any place to go, do you?"

He shakes his head and wishes he can spend the rest of his life in this room, with these two people.

Tom gets down on the floor again to play with his newfound son.

❖   ❖   ❖

Tom lies awake in the darkness. Dim light leaking in from outside the apartment, a combination of the moon's brilliance and several streetlamps, allows his eyes to see. The orange display on the VCR reads 2:15. It has been two hours since Allegra wished him good night. But sleep won't come.

Tommy went to bed hours earlier. Allegra allowed Tom to spend the rest of the day with his son, playing with his toys, watching a couple of Disney videos Tom had never heard of, even eating dinner with the two of them. The day passed by like a thirty-second commercial advertising a better life. Tom never knew when Allegra would finally ask him to leave, but eventually she told him he could sleep on the couch if he wanted to.

He wonders how Allegra can be so forgiving. Or is that the word to use? Has she really forgiven him? Many times Tom wanted to ask Allegra where this was going, what was happening, why she was allowing him to stay, but he forced himself to stop and just enjoy the moment. Every moment. And now that the day is over, Tom's mind can't stop thinking of those moments.

Tom sits up, still wearing his khaki pants and a light T-shirt. His mind machine-guns off another round of pictures from the day: his son taking his hand and showing him where the videos are, eating around a table with Allegra and Tommy, watching Allegra disappear and later emerge in jeans and a T-shirt and her hair down.

This is what you ran away from.

He stands and moves to walk toward the hallway. He doesn't know exactly what he is doing. He just knows he wants to see Allegra. Would she ever take him back? Would she ever allow him to touch her again, in even the slightest way?

Her door is cracked open, and he moves to open it farther. Then he stops himself.

What am I doing?

A moment of panic pierces him. His forehead fills with dots of sweat.

Things aren't like they used to be.

He knows this and turns around, stepping gingerly on the hallway carpet and suddenly hearing a loud creak.

"Tom?" a whisper behind the slit in the door asks.

His heart racing, he turns around and faces the door again, yet says nothing.

"Is that you?"

"Yeah," he whispers back.

A pause, then he hears her say, "You can come in."

He wants to say no, that's quite all right, thanks. But instead he opens the door and enters the small bedroom. He can only make out certain images and shapes in the pitch black of the room.

"Over here," Allegra tells him.

He finds the edge of the mattress and kneels down on

the floor. She lies under the covers on the closest edge of the king-sized bed.

"I couldn't sleep," Tom says.

"Me neither."

"I probably shouldn't be in here."

"Nothing's going to happen," Allegra says.

Tom tries to make her out, but he can't see her.

"I can't imagine what this day has been like for you," she says.

"I'm still trying to process everything."

"I can tell that Tommy likes you."

"Really?"

"Yeah. He never gets like that with men. Not that I have that many around. But still, I've seen him with some guys, and he's usually not that friendly."

"He's a cute kid. Takes after his mother."

"I see you in him every day."

Tom reaches across the bedcover and finds Allegra's face. He strokes one side and remembers how soft her skin is.

"Tom—"

"I just wanted to make sure you're there."

"I'm not going anywhere."

"I wish I could say the same," he replies.

"Listen, I hope I didn't convey the wrong message today."

"No. You didn't."

"I just thought, even after everything, you deserved to see your son. You deserved at least to know what a wonderful boy he is."

"Thank you for letting me stay here."

His mind rushes as he wonders what Allegra is going

to say next.

"I don't really think it's a good idea for you to stick around here after this, though."

"I know," Tom lies.

Silence. Then he hears rustling as Allegra turns on her side and faces him.

"Tom?"

"Yes."

"Why did you leave? What did I do to make you leave?"

He finds her face again and touches it briefly. "You didn't do anything. It was me."

"But if you wanted to leave, why couldn't you have taken me?"

"Allie, I've been wondering that myself. I've been trying to think why I've made such a mess of my life. I can't understand it. I guess I thought I was making a break—a clean break from everything. I guess I thought I needed to do that to start anew."

"A clean break? Is that what you wanted?"

"Maybe. At the time. I don't know. I don't think I knew what I wanted."

"Then tell me—was there ever a time when you loved me?"

Tom clenches his teeth and remembers all the times Allegra told him she loved him. And all the times he never reciprocated. All the times he held his tongue or came up with a clever diversion so he wouldn't have to tell her those words. *I love you.*

"Even after all this time, you still can't say it," Allegra finally says.

"I care about you—I mean, I did care about you."

"It's fine, Tom."

"I don't want to say something I'm unsure about."

"Loving me?"

"Yes. I don't want to lie to you. I'm not sure if I really know the meaning of that word."

"You act like it's a bad word. You can't even say it."

"Allie—"

"Did I pressure you too much? About marriage and about being in love?"

"No."

"Are you sure?"

Her voice is desperate, vulnerable. He could lie to her and perhaps even slide out the L word. Maybe that's all it would take for her to surrender, for her to embrace him and erase six years in one night.

Tom knows better, knows that nothing can expunge those long years. Sleeping together would only make things messier and more wrong.

"I failed," Tom says. "I left you. And I know now it was the biggest mistake I ever made. And I know . . . I know that if I ever loved anybody, it was you."

He finds her face and discovers a tear running down her cheek.

"I shouldn't have come in," he says.

"I'm glad you did."

"Thank you for today."

"You're welcome."

He stands up and wishes her a good night for the second time.

❖   ❖   ❖

By the time they reach the end of the pier, protruding out into the Pacific like a hitchhiker's thumb, Tom realizes where they are. It took them about ten minutes to walk down here, and he thinks at first it's simply a place Allegra enjoys coming. But now he knows why she took him here.

The waves crash, and morning surfers attempt to ride them. White foam and glinting sunshine accent the rich light-blue ocean. The salty smell and the wandering seagulls that drift with the breath of the day remind Tom of another date and time. Another morning the two of them walked out on this pier.

Allegra wears white shorts, tennis shoes, a USC sweatshirt. Her hair is pinned up again, and her eyes hide behind shades. Tom can't help but notice she's taken very good care of herself after having a child.

"I've been here before," Tom says.

"The last place you took me to. Our last date."

Tom is unsure what Allegra wants from him, what she is thinking. This morning as they ate around the table, Allegra seemed distant and quiet. She avoided looking at him directly. She told him she wanted to take him somewhere this morning but didn't say where or why. He thinks he might understand a little better now.

He leans on the railing and stares out to the Pacific.

"The ocean looks limitless."

She glances at him with surprise.

"I've never heard you comment on the ocean."

"I don't think I ever have," he says, his sunglasses aimed toward the rolling waves.

Allegra stands beside him and watches him, almost studying him.

"I used to think it didn't matter," Tom says. "The beauty of everything. You go half a life and never appreciate anything. This is a first—just like so much that has happened to me recently. I wonder why it came so late."

"What?" Allegra asks.

"Appreciating beauty," he says, glancing at her.

"Tom—"

"You know, when that plane went down, I truly thought I was going to die." The waves rush up on the sand behind them, making freshly shadowed lines before withdrawing.

"But you didn't die. Isn't that the point?"

"Would you have cared if I had?"

"How can you say that? Of course I would have cared."

"You have every right to wish me dead."

"I've never wished that, Tom."

She looks so young still, so pure and unjaded.

"At least there's Tommy."

"Meaning?" she asks him.

"If I died, I'd at least have something to show for in this world. I'd have a son."

"I'm glad you know now. I really have wanted to tell you for so long."

Tom takes off his glasses so she can see his eyes.

"I've turned my back on every single person who's ever reached out to me. Especially you."

She turns away from his gaze, stares out toward the ocean.

"Is there any way you can forgive me?"

"I already have," she replies. "Do you think I would've let you spend yesterday with us if I hadn't forgiven you?"

"So is there a chance? Any sort of chance for us?"

"'Us'?"

"I know I can't even begin to ask."

"No, you can't," Allegra says.

"I'm asking anyway."

She gazes into the eternity of the horizon, and Tom wishes he could know what she is thinking.

"When you left me that day on this pier, you didn't tell me much. You barely even said good-bye. I remember thinking for such a long time it was something I did, something I *didn't* do. All this time, I've wondered if you ever loved me."

"Allie—"

"No, please. Just let me talk. You didn't talk years ago. But I'm going to."

She faces him so that her right side faces the ocean. She slips off her glasses so that her piercing eyes can make their impression.

"I used to think that we lived in this fairy-tale sort of world. Living by the ocean, making decent money, having fun. Who needed marriage or anything like that when we had each other? Remember all of our 'If I won the lottery' or 'If I had a million dollars' scenarios? They always included the two of us.

"I really never thought that you could just pick up and leave like that. Even after you brought me out here and told me you were leaving, I always thought you'd come back. Months afterward, when I was showing and walking around by myself with a child living inside of me, I still believed you'd come back. I guess it took me a long time to finally give up."

She takes a deep breath and takes one of Tom's hands. He notices his own hand is shaking.

"I actually thought that morning we came out on this pier—that gorgeous summer day—I actually thought you were going to propose to me."

Allegra laughs and wipes her eyes.

"You want to know something sad, something truly awful? After you showed up the other day, I came back home and barely managed to put Tommy to bed and then spent the entire night bawling like a little girl. You know that?"

"Allie, please—"

She tightens her hands. "But I'm better. It was just the fact that I never thought I'd ever see you again. I never thought you'd ever *want* to see me again. And then there you were."

"I'm sorry."

"I know you are. But, Tom, it doesn't change any-thing. My life is going well. It's not perfect. It's not one of those fairy-tales about living happily ever after that we used to talk about."

"There's no such thing."

"No?" Allegra asks him. "I disagree. I think we had it, you and I. We had it for a while. And you blew it."

"Don't you believe people can change?"

"Some people can, Tom. But I'm not sure that you can."

Tom nods and knows that Allegra might be right.

"I don't know the sort of trouble you're in or what's going to happen to you in the future. And I can't even begin to comprehend what it must be like, surviving a plane crash and all. But I'm no longer responsible for you, Tom. I'm no longer a part of your life. You took that from me years ago on this very same landing. You took that and a lot more."

"I know that."

She still holds his hand, and then she does the unthinkable. She kisses his hand, then stares at it for a long time, finally letting it go.

"I always wanted to hear you propose, to be able to slip a ring over your finger, to know that we were bound by the law and God to each other."

"You believe in God?" Tom asks her.

"I don't know. I'm still unsure in that area, but having a child gives you second thoughts. I'd like Tommy to grow up being grounded, having the same sort of convictions that people like Dale and Lily have."

Tom nods. "Sounds like a smart thing."

"So many things change when you have a child. You know something, Tom? If it was just me here, I wouldn't have a problem taking you back. I mean, I would have some issues, but there might still be a chance. But with Tommy, everything is different."

"What do you mean?"

207

"Do you think I could really allow you to come back into our lives—to come into *his* life—and have you tell him you're his father and allow him to love you and then one day watch you take him out to this pier to say you'll be leaving?"

Wind blows Tom's hair and he shakes his head in disbelief.

"I'd never even think of that."

"Really?" Allegra asks. "Why is that? Because he's your son? Because you love him so much?"

He can't say a word.

Allegra's soft eyes draw tears out of him. Even so, it's not enough to stop her from saying one last thing.

"I love you, Tom. I'll always love you. And one day— one long day from now—you'll realize why you should have loved me."

She turns without hesitation and begins walking the hundred meters back to land, back to her home and her son and her life. Tom watches her fading outline until he cannot see it anymore.

❖   ❖   ❖

A quivering finger dials the number. He needs to hear someone's voice, and he's already tried Dale and Lily's house twice to no avail. No recording machine, no anything. So he's trying to see if he can locate Sean. He's tried his brother's room but gotten nothing except a hotel-room voice mail message he doesn't believe. So he's trying his only other option.

He listens to the ringer on his cell phone he left with Sean in Vegas.

Once.

Twice.

"Yeah?"

"Sean?"

"Tom! Is that you?"

A voice that sounds more desperate than his own shouts at him.

"Where are you?"

A jumbled jargon of curses and ranting makes Tom ask his brother what's wrong.

"Tom—man, listen to me. Dale and Lily. I can't—it's not my fault—everything—" then more cursing and blaspheming God.

"What's wrong, Sean? Where're Dale and Lily?"

"They're dead, Tom. I've been trying to get hold of you, but I had no idea where you were."

"What?"

"They're dead. The cops called me—they're dead, Tom. Dale and Lily."

Choking. Tom feels his throat close, the heat of the day grab him in a stranglehold, the madness of the past week finally climaxing.

"No—"

"Where are you?" Sean asks.

"California. I came out to see Allegra." He feels numb, weightless, empty.

"Tom?"

"What happened? Are you sure?"

"I'm in the Springs now, Tom. The cops are here. They called me, and I came right out here. They found them yesterday, Tom. They're wanting to talk to you."

"How—"

"They were shot. At home in their beds."

Dear God above, if you're there this isn't happening. This cannot be happening, not after everything else. . . . Why, God . . . oh dear God, why?

"Sean, listen—"

"Is this—does this have anything to do with—"

"No."

"Those guys? Sloan? All of that? Is it—I mean, I didn't say anything."

"Sean?"

"Yeah?"

"Are you okay?"

"Yeah, I'm fine."

"Sean, I'm sorry."

"What?"

"This is all my fault."

"Don't say that, man. I didn't know how to reach you. I've been trying, and I took your phone but I didn't know—"

Sean blurts out his words a mile a minute, just like he always does when he's nervous. And slightly drunk or high.

Tom stares out and can see the ocean from the phone booth where he's standing. An hour after Allegra left him on the pier, he discovers he's truly alone in this world.

He feels guilt. And horror. And pain. But most of all, he feels empty. He feels alone.

"Where are you?" Tom asks Sean.

Sean tells him he's at a bar in the Springs. The police questioned him all day yesterday.

"Don't go anywhere and don't do anything. Okay?"

"What's wrong? What happened? Do you really think it was—"

"Yes," Tom interrupts. "And just like every miserable thing that's wrong, it's all my fault."

"Don't say that, man. I mean, I—"

"I'm going to get on the first plane I can, and I'll be out there soon. Just be careful. I'll call you when I know my itinerary."

"Tom, I'm so sorry."

Sean begins to wail over the phone, and Tom tells him to hang in there. He tells him to get control of himself and that he'll call him soon.

He hangs up the phone and finds his hand still shaking.

It is truly over.

All of it.

❖ ❖ ❖

The world rushes by as he drives toward the airport. He passes a Taco Bell and a Wal-Mart and a bank and a grocery store and the greens turn to yellow and then to red and the cars surround him and stop and go and everything goes on just as it always does, yet Tom knows it's all over. He knows that his life—his worthless, selfish, miserable life—is finally coming to a conclusion. No matter what happens and where he goes and what he does, he can never have it back. The tiny bit of *good* that was in his life is gone now.

He passes a church and sees the small white sign on the curb that announces a meeting time and then contains the blurb of the day:

"Our unknown future is known to God."

Tom lets out an angry gasp. He grips the steering wheel while the rest of the world begins to turn slightly. His eyes narrow, and he feels a wave thunder into him. He pulls over in a parking lot of a fast-food restaurant, opens the car door, and unleashes a day's worth of food all over the blacktop pavement. His eyes water and his nose is clogged and he vomits again, then spits out the junk in his mouth and wipes it and sits back in his car in delirium.

"What's it going to be, God?" he screams. "What do you have in store next? Huh? What's next?"

Tom finally puts the car in drive and heads down the street. All he can think about is that sign, as if the sign is the one thing he can vent his anger toward.

Maybe there is a God, he finds himself thinking. He actually wants there to be a God. An all-controlling, all-knowing God. Because then he can dump all this anger and intensity on him. Then he can find the one true person to blame.

Did you do all of this? Did you allow this to happen? Are you really up there, and do you even care one bit?

He drives and feels glad to have thrown up. Rather that than get on a plane and do it.

Tom thinks of traveling on a plane. Suddenly the thought of going down doesn't haunt him. It actually makes him laugh. That would be a grand finale, a fitting close to this horror story. He gets back on a plane and it goes down.

"How's that sound to you?" he shouts above the wind and the noise from the stereo. "Pretty cool ending, huh?"

He wipes his face and realizes his cheeks are wet from tears he didn't know he was crying.

❖ ❖ ❖

Tom sits in a plastic waiting room with the ticket in his hand. It cost over a thousand dollars, but he didn't think twice about spending the money. Cost means nothing to him anymore.

He waits. Only twenty minutes before boarding. He's called his brother and told him what time he will be arriving in Colorado Springs. And he's gained a little more control over his voice, over his actions, over his body. At least he's no longer crying or throwing up.

He watches nameless and faceless people pass. He wonders how wonderful their lives are and how different his turned out to be.

He stares at the name on the ticket.

Tom Ledger. Same as always. How could it be the same when everything is so different?

He looks at the ticket and notes the departure time—Wednesday, 4:45 P.M. The date on the ticket is June 28.

So much can happen in just a week's time. Everything changes with a simple turn of the breath. A cough, and your life is over.

He was foolish and ignorant to think he could have his dreams fulfilled. To think the people he was dealing with weren't violent or dangerous. To think things could have turned out good.

The ticket in his hand feels heavy as a new thought hits him.

What would have happened if I had died in that plane crash?

Nothing. None of this would have happened. Dale and Lily would still be alive. Allegra wouldn't have been hurt by his momentary appearance in her life. Sean wouldn't be in danger.

I should have never taken that deal in the first place.

Tom remembers Pastor Marks sitting next to him. It feels like a lifetime ago, an eternity.

He should have lived, not me.

Staring at the ticket, he keeps seeing his name.

"God—" he begins, this time not saying it as a curse but as a plea.

"He deserved to live. I deserved to die."

He continues to stare at the ticket and wonders why he was allowed to live, if living is what this is actually called. He was given a second chance, yet he did nothing with it. Instead, he erased every decent thing left in his life.

He waits until they begin the boarding call, then stands in line and waits to step onto the plane.

❖   ❖   ❖

The plane is a smaller craft, the kind with only five seats across—two on one side of the aisle and three on the other side. Tom gets his usual "B" seat, an aisle seat with a window seat next to him, and then closes his eyes and wonders how his brother will be. And what the police will do.

What will they ask me? And what will I tell them?

Does it matter anymore, even if he goes to prison? Could anything be worse than the hell he's living in now?

Maybe it's time to tell the truth.

Tom opens his eyes and looks out through the oval window, noticing the sleek wing shining in the afternoon sunlight.

He hears an apologetic voice and absently looks up to see a man struggling with a large piece of luggage, trying to fit it in the overhead bin.

"Sorry," the man says to the line behind him.

Tom squints his eyes and looks up in confusion. The man finally faces forward and Tom gets a glimpse of his face and his breathing stops.

The stranger wears a cordial grin even though he knows he's holding up the line.

What?

A carrying case slips off the man's shoulder and lands in Tom's lap.

"Oh, sorry. Excuse me."

Wait a minute here.

But of course, he's just drifted off and his mind is dreaming, recalling his first meeting with Pastor Marks.

But I'm awake. Wide awake.

Tom says nothing but takes the black canvas bag, the sort they hand out free at conventions, and puts it in the aisle. He notices the inscription on the front of the bag: "Riverside Bible Church."

"Sir, we'll need to store that in the back," a flight attendant tells the man. The row of travelers behind him has grown, and irritated glares pierce his back.

This can't be happening—not like it all did before.

"Sorry, I thought it'd fit," he says with an apologetic smile.

Tom shuts his eyes and opens them again. Then again. Then a third time. Nothing changes. He is still locked in to the same dream.

Wake up. Wake up, Tom.

"Thank you. I'm really sorry."

The brown-haired man picks up his shoulder bag and looks at his ticket stub. He appears confused as Tom stands to let him in. He slides into the window seat, apologizing again while Tom says nothing.

The man wiggles in his seat, looking out the window and then staring at his ticket stub. He clears his throat.

"Um, excuse me?" he says to Tom.

Tom looks at him and wants to say something to Kent Marks, this friendly man he once wanted to ignore. He wants to say something but can't, feels his voice and his vocal cords shut off.

"You know, the travel agent told me this was going to be an aisle seat. I guess I should've checked, huh? I don't fly much."

Tom continues to stare at him, saying nothing. He can't say anything.

That's because I'm dreaming and soon, very soon, I'm going to wake up.

"Would it be a big deal to switch?"

Wake up.

Tom looks down and sees that he is wearing dress slacks and a buttoned shirt. He notes the $350 black shoes he's wearing and thought were ruined in the plane accident. Suddenly he hears Kent Marks talking to him.

". . . but I've been battling a bad stomach thing—I mean, it's not contagious or anything. I just worry—I might need to take a quick trip to the bathroom."

The man looks at him, still wanting to change seats.

Tom looks at his hands and digs the thumbnail into his palm. Pain. He feels his face and notes it's freshly shaved.

"Could you tell me the time?" Tom asks Kent.

"Excuse me?" the man asks, confused.

"What time is it?"

"It's about—well, let's see. It's 10:32."

"In the morning?" Tom asks.

The man, more innocent and friendly looking than Tom remembers, blinks with curiosity and then tells him yes.

"You okay?" he questions.

Tom nods. Then he asks, "What's today?"

"What do you mean?"

"The date?"

"Are you serious?" Kent asks him.

"The date—seriously."

"It's June 20."

The last passengers file past, and the attendant begins to make sure everyone is seated. Tom just stares numbly at the man next to him.

"So can we switch? I'm sorry to ask, but I really—"

Tom nods his head and says it's fine. He steps up and allows the man to slide out to the aisle. Tom takes the seat by the window and feels his stomach drop as he buckles in and looks outside to see the large wing of a 767.

"You a nervous flyer too?" Kent Marks asks him as he buckles in next to him.

"Why do you say that?"

"Oh, nothing. Just, you look a bit pale."

"I haven't had the best luck in flights recently."

"Really?"

Tom nods, saying nothing more.

"It's been years since I've flown," Kent tells him.

Yeah, you already told me that once.

The attendant's voice comes over the intercom, and Tom notes how calm her voice sounds, how different from her screams of "Brace yourself! Brace yourself!" But it's the same voice he heard before.

"All portable electronic devices must be turned off—"

And as she continues, Tom suddenly remembers his cell phone. It's there, just like his wallet and everything else that he needs.

He pulls it out so suddenly that Kent Marks looks at him with surprise.

"Excuse me," he says, turning on the phone and finding Dale and Lily's number on the names stored inside.

He calls them up and on the third ring, a serene Aunt Lily answers.

"Hello?"

"Lily?"

"Yes?"

"Is that really you?"

"Yes. Is this Tom?"

"Yes, it's me."

"Are you okay?" she asks.

"I'm fine. Listen to me. What is today?"

"What?"

"The date? What's today's date?"

He glances over at Kent, and the man next to him shrugs as if saying *I already told you.*

"It's June 20, I believe. Well, let me think—yes, that's right."

He lets out a sigh.

This is a dream, and you're gonna wake up.

"Lily, are you okay? How's Dale?"

"He's fine. Where are you?"

"I'm calling from a plane."

"You are? How come?"

"I'm flying to Colorado Springs."

Tom feels a nudge and looks up to see Kent shake his head. "This is going to San Francisco. Are you on the right flight?"

Tom laughs, then nods. "Sorry, Lily. I mean—I'm heading to San Francisco."

An attendant steps up next to him and politely asks him to turn off his phone. He holds up a hand to tell her just a minute.

"Listen, Lily. Are you going to be there for a while?"

"Well, yes. I mean, we were thinking about going to Sam's for a while, but—"

"No, no, no, no," he rattles off quickly. "Don't go anywhere. Okay? Please. Just—wait for me to call you back. Okay?"

Her voice is puzzled. "Well, all right."

"Talk with you soon."

He turns off the phone and clips it shut.

"What is it?" the bewildered stranger asks. Or is he a stranger since Tom knows him?

"What is what?"

"You. You're smiling."

"I am? Yeah, I guess so."

"Are you okay?" Kent asks.

Tom says he is and holds out his hand. "I'm Tom. Tom Ledger."

And if this is a dream, I don't want to wake up.

"Nice to meet you, Tom. Thanks for switching seats. I'm Kent Marks."

They shake hands and Tom thinks, *It's good to see you again.*

Tom keeps shutting his eyes and then opening them hard to make sure he's not dreaming. But part of him knows this isn't a dream. He can't say what it is, but it's not a dream.

As the plane jostles to the runway, Tom makes sure his belt buckle is tightened.

You switched seats.

He looks out the window and sees the wing and looks up toward the clear blue skies.

This feels right, whatever happens from here.

Tom tries to think back over what happened in the past twenty-four hours. If they really were the last twenty-four hours.

He remembers what he said in the airport waiting room.

His prayer. His second official prayer.

Was it heard? Could it really have been heard? And answered?

As the plane soars up to the heavens, Tom hears one phrase running through his head over and over.

You are my hiding place.

Y ou have very cute kids," Tom says.

"Thanks. I think so."

They've been in the air only fifteen minutes, and Tom continues to talk with Kent. He's almost afraid that if he stops, this whole reality will turn into a blurry dream and he'll find himself alone again.

"How 'bout you? Have any children?"

Tom nods and finds it strange to acknowledge. "A son."

"Really? How old?"

"Five. I—I've only seen him once. I left my girlfriend years ago."

Kent's face is visibly surprised.

"Stupid thing for me to do," Tom continues. "I think I know that now."

There is a pause, and Tom stares out the window again and the clouds below them.

"We've all made mistakes," says Kent Marks.

"You can say that too?" Tom asks.

"Of course. It's only by God's grace that I haven't made more."

"God's grace? Meaning?"

"His mercy. His favor. How I ever ended up becoming a pastor—that's an example of his grace."

"How so?" Tom asks, intrigued.

"My parents weren't Christians, so I grew up doing my own thing. I lived in northern Michigan. I had no connection to church until my senior year of high school, when my best friend died in a car accident. He was one of those guys, you know—the most popular in the school, homecoming king, jock, everything going for him. It really messed me up, his death. I decided after his funeral service where they spoke about the hope of heaven that I'd go to church again."

"And you've been going ever since?"

"The second time I went I walked down the aisle. You know, went down to the front of the church for the altar call. I used to laugh when I saw people doing that. But I needed to go, needed to talk to a pastor. I accepted Christ that spring Sunday when I was a senior."

Tom nods and wants to say something but averts his attention when the airline attendant asks him what he wants to drink. He orders a soda and watches Kent do the same.

He sips the cup of 7UP and wonders, *Will anything about this trip change? Is it still going to go down again?*

He notices small things—the people across the aisle from him, the attendant's gestures and smiles and words, the sound of a baby somewhere behind him. All of these mirror the last flight.

The only difference is you're in Kent's seat.

Maybe it was meant for him all along.

Tom turns to Kent and resumes the conversation. He is filled with questions he wants to ask this young man of faith, this solid example who died leaving a family behind and a church proclaiming his praises.

"Have you ever had doubts since then?"

"Doubts? About God? Not really. I mean, there are times I don't understand why he allows something to happen. I'll see something on the news and wonder why. But no, my faith has grown over the years."

"Interesting."

"You go to church?" Kent asks.

"My aunt and uncle do. I lived with them after my father passed away."

"And do you share their beliefs?"

Tom chuckles, but it's not a mean-spirited cynical chuckle like he would have let out a week earlier—the kind he probably did let out on this exact same date when it occurred the first time. This time it's simply an honest and bewildered laugh.

"No. Not exactly. But a lot's happened the last few days."

"How so?"

"Long story," Tom says. "Just—well, I actually prayed twice. Recently, that is. And both times, my prayers were answered."

"I'm not surprised by that."

Kent's smile is contagious.

"Earphones?" the brown-haired attendant asks them.

"No thanks," Tom says, reflecting with dark humor that no one is going to finish watching the movie anyway.

Kent declines the earphones too. Tom pops his ears and marvels at the smooth flight of the plane.

What if everything was a dream? The crash and the

old man named Earl and driving to the Springs and being there with Lily and Dale.

He suddenly reaches for his cell phone again and turns it on. Then, thinking about Kent, he offers an explanation.

"Hey—I don't mean to cut our conversation short. I just—I need to call someone quickly."

Kent signals that he doesn't mind while Tom presses redial and hears Aunt Lily's sweet voice answer the phone again.

"Tom, what's wrong?" she instantly asks when she hears his voice.

"Nothing. I promise. Could you—Is Dale around?"

"He's here."

"Put him on the other line."

"How come?"

"I just—I just felt it might be good to talk to both of you."

Lily puts the receiver down and calls out for Dale. While he waits for them to come to the phone, Tom looks around at his fellow passengers. They are talking, sleeping, reading, doing all the usual things people do on an airplane. They can't see the urgency in Tom, the racing of his heart, the slow and building throb in the back of his throat. He knows what's about to occur, what's going to happen, and no one else knows. As far as every single soul on this plane goes, they're all looking forward to tonight and tomorrow and the rest of their lives.

I got a glimpse of the rest of mine, Tom thinks with horror. *And it didn't look pretty.*

"Hi, Tom," Uncle Dale says.

"Hey, guys. I just wanted to call—it's been a while, I know."

"How are you doing?" Lily asks.

"I'm fine. Doing okay."

"You're on a business trip?"

"Yes. Sort of. Look, could I ask you a question—and just be honest?"

"Yeah," Lily says quickly.

"Allegra. When did you last hear from her?"

A silence for a moment, so Tom continues.

"Look, I know about Allegra. And Tommy."

"What?" Lily asks. "Did you see them?"

So it is true. I didn't imagine Allegra and my son.

"No."

"How do you know?"

"When did you last hear from them?" Tom asks.

"Last Christmas—I got a card. And a couple of pictures."

"Are they doing well?"

"They're doing good," Uncle Dale answers when Lily can't.

"That's good to know."

"You should see them sometime," Lily says. "It's been so long. And you haven't talked about her for such a long while."

"I've done a lot of things I wished I could change. But listen, I want you two to know—I love you. In my own way, whatever that is."

"Tom?"

"I know it sounds crazy for me to call and tell you that."

"What's wrong?" Lily asks again.

"It's just—I was thinking—if something happened and I was never given a second chance to say those words. I wanted to make sure you knew."

"We love you too," Lily says. Her voice sounds tight.

"If something ever happened to me, would you keep an eye on Allegra and Tommy?"

"Of course," Dale replies. "We already do."

Tom smiles.

"You need to come visit us soon," Lily says.

"I will. I'll try my best as soon as I finish up in San Fran."

"Thank you for calling."

"You guys take care."

Tom shuts off the phone and looks out the window. He feels a sadness inside of him and wonders if he'll actually be able to go through all of this.

Again.

He breathes in and shuts his eyes, though he knows he is far from sleeping.

And seconds later, a fierce blast rocks the plane. He opens his eyes and looks out the window to his left, then turns to see Kent grabbing both arms of his seat and looking toward the right side of the plane.

"What was that?" Kent asks above the shouts and mumbles inside the plane.

Tom looks at him and says he doesn't know and that it didn't sound good. He feels the plane begin to descend.

Here we go.

❖   ❖   ❖

Honey, things will be fine. I promise you. Don't —come on, don't. It's okay. Listen, it will be fine. I just wanted to call—I didn't want to worry you. I just wanted to call."

Tom sees Kent wipe the tears away and all of a sudden, the most bizarre thing happens. He realizes it's crazy, that all of this is crazy, that the past few hours have been lifted from some bizarre *Twilight Zone* episode. Soon Rod Serling will come and begin talking about Tom Ledger in a droll voice while smoking a cigarette. The whole thing is surreal. And yet, Tom listens to Kent tell his wife that he loves her and to just pray, and Tom feels a thrill rush through him.

Things will be fine, Tom thinks and believes. *For you guys.*

He finds himself strangely content after hearing the phone conversation between Kent and his wife. Everything is happening exactly like it did earlier. Tom is simply sitting in a different seat.

Tom and Kent discuss the Marks family. Tom tries to keep Kent focused on his family and tries to reassure him that things will be okay.

"It's Tom, right?" Kent asks.

"Yes."

"Tom, are you a praying man?"

"Not really," Tom replies.

"Well, I was just wondering if you wanted to pray with me. You said earlier you had recently prayed."

"That's right."

"For the first time ever?"

"I think so."

"And your prayers were answered?"

"Do you really think they could have been? Can someone who's never believed in God actually have a prayer answered?"

"Of course. God can do anything."

"Yeah, but why would he do anything for someone who doesn't even believe in him?"

"Do you know about Saul?"

"No," Tom says.

"He was an angry man who persecuted the early Christians. He hated them. Then, on the road to Damascus, God stopped him in his tracks and blinded him, asking him why he was doing all of these things."

"So Saul got what was coming to him?"

"God *saved* him. And he went on to become the apostle Paul. You've heard of him, right?"

Tom nods.

"Saul's story shows us that God can change anyone, no matter what we've done to him."

The plane lurches and shifts right, and Kent breathes in deeply and moans a bit.

"Yeah, but what if God doesn't do the bright lights and the talking-from-heaven bit? What if it's just left up to us? When is there ever a good time?"

Kent directs intense eyes on Tom, as if he's suddenly realized what's going on with him.

"Tom—I waited almost eighteen years before I gave my life to Christ. I wished I hadn't waited that long."

"What about after thirty-four years? After believing in no one but myself all that time?"

"Tom, there is never too late a time to come to the Lord. Do you know that when they crucified Christ, when he was dying on a cross, they crucified two thieves right next to him? One of them cursed Jesus. The other asked Jesus to remember him when he died. And Jesus told him that he would be with him that day in heaven."

"What'd he have to do?"

"He believed, Tom. He believed and was sorry for the mistakes he'd made."

Kent's turquoise eyes reveal their compassion and belief at the same time.

"Is there a way you could pray for me?" Tom asks.

"What do you mean?"

"I'm afraid that if I die, I won't be like that thief. That I will end up, well, somewhere else."

"Tom, you don't need me to pray for you. You need to pray yourself."

"What for?"

"You need to ask God to save you."

"For this plane?"

Kent shakes his head. "From your sin. Ask for Christ's forgiveness. Do you believe that he died on the cross?"

"I really don't know—at this point, I'm not sure—I just—I do believe there's a God."

"So you need to pray to him. You need to ask for his forgiveness."

The plane rattles, and the pressure seems loud. Tom and Kent ignore the passing attendants, the occasional message over the intercom, the crying passengers.

"I just—how could he—why would he want to forgive me?" Tom asks.

"He sent his Son to die for you. And for the world."

Tom thinks of his own son and wonders how any father could ever do such a thing. How could he give up the one and only thing that belonged to him?

"Tom, we're going to be landing soon."

"I know this is all—it feels so corny," Tom says.

"What do you feel in your heart?" Kent asks him.

"I feel sorry. I wish that—I wish I could've been like you. I wish I could have known all this when I was eighteen."

"Tell that to God. Pray out loud. Or silently."

Tom turns to the outside sky and wonders if God can hear him. He doesn't think as he begins to pray again to the same God who answered his earlier prayers, the God who allowed him to live thirty-four years and finally find the truth of the ages at the end of that short life. He feels afraid and humbled, but mostly he feels relieved.

His voice prays out loud.

"Dear God, wherever you are, thank you for hearing my earlier prayers. And I ask that you hear this one too. I ask for your forgiveness, that you remember me when all of this is over with. I ask that you save me, even though I don't understand so much about what that means. I ask for your mercy, God. I believe in you and your Son, and I don't understand or know what's going to happen. I'm scared, God. I'm sorry for my life."

Images shoot through his head. Dale and Lily. Sean. Allegra. Tommy.

"I apologize for my sorry life. For all those I hurt. For all those I'm leaving behind without asking for their forgiveness. For only living for myself."

"Tom, can I pray for us now?" Kent asks with tears in his eyes.

Tom nods. He feels exhausted, yet he is not scared anymore. Kent's words lifted his spirits.

"Dear heavenly Father, I thank and praise your name for giving Tom a second chance, for opening his eyes and allowing you into his heart. I pray for Tom and for the rest of us, Lord. I pray that you bring us safely down and that you give us long and fulfilling lives where we can praise your holy name. I ask for your mercy on all of us as sinners, Lord, and I thank you that you did send your Son to die for us. Thank you for your unfailing love and for the fact that we can come to you no matter what mistakes we've made or how long we've lived apart from you.

"Lord, please give us hope and faith in these next few moments. I ask this in your precious Son's name, Amen."

Kent taps Tom on the shoulder.

"We're going to make it through this," he says. "You're going to have a long life ahead of you."

The plane bounces and Kent lurches forward, banging his head against the tray table in front of him.

"Even if it's a rough landing."

The captain's voice comes on the intercom. Just like it did the first time.

"Folks, this is Captain Younter again. We're about four minutes from touching down. Everyone needs to be in position, with heads down—"

Four minutes.

God can do whatever he wants.

Does that mean he will save Tom?

He's already saved me, Tom thinks. He is surprised to realize he believes it. He's surprised that he's not panicking or feeling sick or fearing his death. He knows that anything can happen.

Tom thinks of calling Allegra but knows there's no time now. He remembers her address but not her home phone number. The plane continues to shake as Tom reaches for a pen in his shirt pocket.

"Do you have any paper?"

"What for?" Kent says, his forehead sweaty and his face colorless. But he looks in his bag and comes up with several sheets of notebook paper on a clipboard.

"This okay?"

"Yes, thanks."

Tom begins to write as quickly as he can, writing from his heart, hoping the words will find their way to Allegra.

My dearest Allegra,

I am writing in the hope that these words get to you. If they do, you'll know that my plane went down and I didn't make it.

I want to tell you I've now seen a tiny glimpse of the life I could have had with you. And I need you to know that I know about Tommy. I know he's a good kid and that you're an incredible mother. I know you'll love him the rest of your life in a way I never possibly could.

My thoughts are jumbled—so much to say—

You need to know this, Allegra. I left you years ago because I was afraid. I was afraid that I was missing out on something bigger the world had to offer. I knew there was something I needed. I just didn't realize exactly what that was, what I was looking for. I finally understand it now. I've found the hope I was looking for.

I know I might not be making sense. But maybe the man I give this letter to—maybe he can explain things better. I don't have the time and ability. Just know that I am truly sorry for leaving you and I know I can never ever make it up to you. I know I can never take away the pain and hurt. But I want you to know I didn't leave because of anything you did or didn't do. You were wonderful. I was the one who wasn't enough.

I never had the courage to tell you how I felt. But I know that I loved you, Allegra. And I still love you. I love you with my whole heart and being and every inch of me. And I wish so desperately that I could tell you that in person. But, as with so many things in my life, I won't be able to make amends for that. I'm trying to at least right the biggest wrong I made in my life—failing to let you know how much I loved you.

Sorry for the scribbled line above—the plane just took a major dip. What I wrote was that I loved you, that I love you still. I can picture you in that wonderful, intimate apartment with Tommy.

No matter what happens, please know there is hope—I've found it. You know me. I once refused to even ponder the question of whether there was a God. But now I know God's always been there, just waiting. Waiting for me to stop failing and finally come to him.

If I never see you again, and if this letter does find you, know that I did love you, Allegra. I'll always love you. And I pray that the same angels who watched over me will watch over you and Tommy.

Good-bye,
Tom

He folds up the letter and gives it to Kent, who for the time being is scrunched up with his head near his knees.

"Kent, you're going to make it through this," Tom tells him.

Kent breathes in and lets out a sigh.

"Listen. If I don't make it out of this, can you give this to the mother of my son? Her name and address are on the top of the letter."

Kent takes the letter and squints his eyes, not understanding.

"If you don't survive the landing, I'm not sure what's going to happen to me," Kent says.

Tom nods. "I know. This is just—just in case."

"Well, okay. I will. I promise."

"Thanks," says Tom.

For everything.

The plane shakes, and the attendants shout for everyone to brace themselves. Tom hears the sound of the crying baby and coughing and voices mumbling, perhaps praying. The sound of the engines screams outside as the wounded plane plunges downward. Tom leans in his seat and stares at his $350 shoes and the floor and feels the jerking and the velocity and speaks a prayer out loud.

"God, remember me."

He closes his eyes. And waits.

And Jesus replied, "Today you will be with me in Paradise."

Luke 23:43

S INCE 1894, Moody Publishers has been dedicated to equip and motivate people to advance the cause of Christ by publishing evangelical Christian literature and other media for all ages, around the world. As a ministry of the Moody Bible Institute of Chicago, proceeds from the sale of this book help to train the next generation of Christian leaders.

If we may serve you in any way in your spiritual journey toward understanding Christ and the Christian life, please contact us at www.moodypublishers.com.

"All Scripture is God-breathed and is useful for teaching, rebuking, correcting and training in righteousness, so that the man of God may be thoroughly equipped for every good work."
—2 TIMOTHY 3:16, 17

MOODY
PUBLISHERS

THE NAME YOU CAN TRUST

THE SECOND THIEF TEAM

ACQUIRING EDITOR:
Michele Straubel

COPY EDITOR:
Ann Buchanan

BACK COVER COPY:
Julie-Allyson Ieron, Joy Media

COVER DESIGN:
Barb Fisher, LeVan Fisher Design

INTERIOR DESIGN:
Ragont Design

PRINTING AND BINDING:
Dickinson Press Inc.

The typeface for the text of this book is
Caslon 224

Travis welcomes emails sent to him at
TT@Tyndale.com. For more information on him, you
may visit www.TravisThrasher.com.

From Dust and Ashes

ISBN: 0-8024-1554-7

Nazis flee under cover of darkness as American troops near the town of St. Georgen. A terrible surprise awaits the unsuspecting GIs. And three people - the wife of an SS guard, an American soldier, and a concentration camp survivor -- will never be the same.

Inspired by actual events surrounding the liberation of a Nazi concentration camp, *From Dust and Ashes* shows the healing power of forgiveness.

What a story! It sweeps us back to a time when the world swore "Never again" and gives us raw hope to walk away with.
Anne De Graaf, International best-selling author & Christy Award winner.

The Brother's Keeper

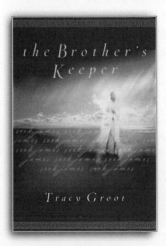

ISBN: 0-8024-3105-4

Thirty years after he followed a star to Bethlehem, one of the Magi is back on another mission. This time, he is sent not to an infant "king of the Jews," but to the king's brother James.

The sons of Joseph run a successful carpentry business in Nazareth. At least, it was successful until the oldest brother, Jesus, left home to tell the world He will forgive their sins and save their souls. Now everyone is hearing outlandish reports of healings and exorcisms. Business is suffering; not many people want a stool made by the family of the local crazy man.

Valkyries Book 1
Some through the Fire

Streetwise freshman Tracey Jacamuzzi knows that if anyone discovers the whole truth about her, they'll give up on her entirely. She isn't so sure they'd be wrong.

This is where Tracey's story begins - but certainly not where it ends. Because God has set His sights on this young woman. And His plan is to use all of her experiences to draw her to Himself. Along the way, He enlists the help of some unlikely friends.

ISBN 0-8024-1513-X

Valkyries Book 2
All through the Blood

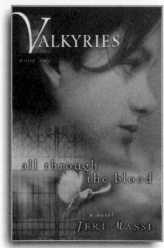

Most days, life seems more like a prison than an adventure to Tracey Jacumuzzi. She feels more like a failure than a Valkyrie. And it's no wonder. Her junior year is marred by her parent's divorce, the death of a classmate, and the continued violence of a fellow basketball player.

Tracey's faith in Christ is growing, and she is achieving excellence as an athlete. But she can't seem to control her own actions or rise above her violent past. Even at her lowest point, she begins to understand the potent mercy of the God who refuses to give up on her.

ISBN 0-8024-1514-8

MOODY
PUBLISHERS
THE NAME YOU CAN TRUST.

1-800-678-6928 www.MoodyPublishers.com